REVENGE AT RAWHIDE

In every waking moment, U.S. Deputy Marshal Dan Casey is haunted by the flames — and the laughter. It has been twelve years since the outlaws killed his parents and sister and left him for dead in that cellar. When Dan returns to Rawhide, no one recognizes him, and that suits him just fine. The good citizens are eager to help him clean up the town — but how much more blood will be spilled before the outlaws are brought to justice?

Books by Lee Phillips
in the Linford Western Library:

FURY AT SWEETWATER PASS
THE LONE RIDER

LEE PHILLIPS

REVENGE AT RAWHIDE

Complete and Unabridged

LINFORD
Leicester

First published in the
United States of America

Originally published under the
name of 'Lee Martin'

First Linford Edition
published 2000

All the characters in this book are fictitious,
and any resemblance to actual persons,
living or dead, is purely coincidental.

British Library CIP Data

Phillips, Lee
  Revenge at Rawhide.—Large print ed.—
Linford western library
  1. Western stories
  2. Large type books
  I. Title
  823.9'14 [F]

  ISBN 0–7089–5909–1

Published by
F. A. Thorpe (Publishing)
Anstey, Leicestershire

Set by Words & Graphics Ltd.
Anstey, Leicestershire
Printed and bound in Great Britain by
T. J. International Ltd., Padstow, Cornwall

This book is printed on acid-free paper

To my lovely mother for her
wisdom, joy,
inspiration, and gentle,
unfailing support.

1

In the afternoon sun, Dan Casey reined his black stallion to a halt. He leaned on the pommel and gazed down at the ruins of the isolated ranch house. Painful memories shot through him.

In his pocket was a letter posted from the town of Rawhide that began, *I know who did it. Get here as fast as you can.*

Grimly, he pushed his wide-brimmed Stetson back from his damp brow and looked around at the eastern foothills rimmed by the distant Colorado Rockies. It was spring of 1879. He was all of twenty-seven and wearing a new badge on his black leather vest, a circled star that read *United States Deputy Marshal*.

The air was cold and clean, blown at him by a rising wind. His rugged, weathered face showed the tension of the years spent planning this ride. He had ice-blue eyes, a tight mouth, and square jaw. His dark-brown hair was cropped at the collar. His wide shoulders and lean body rode tall in the saddle. At his right hip, an Army Colt was well-oiled and ready. A Winchester repeater hung in his scabbard.

He slowly dismounted and stood at the edge of the ruins. Only the stone chimney remained, rising among the fallen timbers. The scene unfurled painfully before him.

He had been fifteen years old. With his seven-year-old sister, Ann, he slept in the loft at the rear of the house. One night, they were awakened by rifle fire and a weird laugh outside their window. He scrambled from his bed, seized his small rifle, and hurried down the ladder, his frightened sister at his heels.

'Pa!' he had yelled.

Then he saw his father, Tom Cassidy, kneeling over their fallen, lifeless mother, blood on her back. The big man rose at sight of them and shoved

2

them down to the floor. Rifle fire shattered the windows and hammered at the walls. Smoke poured from the ceiling, its boards already smoldering as flames licked down the front wall, hot and furious.

His father was bleeding at the chest, and Dan reached up for him. At that moment, a bullet slammed into Dan's left shoulder, knocking him down like a club.

The rifle fire and the hideous laugh outside became as one, thundering through the smoke in a deafening roar.

His father crawled to his sister and thrust her down into the open cellar trapdoor. He motioned to Dan to follow.

Believing his father would come with them, Dan dragged himself and his rifle to the opening, dropping down into the black hole, where his sister was sobbing in the dark. Dan frantically lit the lamp. But when the cellar door suddenly closed down tight overhead, he knew his father was trying to save them while fighting it out to the end.

'Pa,' he yelled. 'Let me help you!'

Bleeding and in pain, Dan clawed at the trapdoor, but his father had blocked it. Smoke curled down from the floor above. He tried to open the outside cellar door at the back of the house, but it was stuck.

He called to his father even as smoke filled the cellar. Holding his sobbing, gasping sister in his arms, he begged her to stay alive while he gripped his rifle with his free hand, blood running down his left arm.

Tears stung Dan's eyes as he stared at the ruins, the memories close and painful.

Suddenly, his reverie was interrupted by a sound that brought him hurtling back to the present. It was a woman's scream, and it came from the north, near the distant Wild River. He remembered the spot as a popular one for picnics; a sheltered, shaded rise where wildflowers grew. He mounted, spun his stallion, and set it into a

4

gallop, crossing the green expansion in record time.

As he reined up on the rise, he looked down at the shallow water of the river, which was sixty feet wide at this bend. A gray horse and buggy were tied in a grove of cottonwoods. Two bays were nearby, ground-tied and nipping at each other. A picnic had been laid out in the shade with a red-and-white checkered tablecloth. Pretty little dishes were set near a basket.

A young, blond man in a fancy blue coat was on his knees, a six-gun held to his head by a scruffy cowhand with a cigarette dangling from his fat mouth. The gunman was obviously intoxicated.

Down by the river, a woman in a green dress was struggling with a stocky man in a black hat. He was holding her against him, his mouth fighting to reach hers. Her golden hair was thrown in every direction as she tried to avoid his kiss.

Dan started his stallion down the slope, hand on his holster.

The man and woman fell to the ground and rolled as she screamed, pounding at his head with her fist. Then she shoved a handful of dirt in his mouth. He gasped, coughing and spitting, and fell on hands and knees.

The young woman scrambled to her feet. Lifting her skirts to her ankles, she placed a small boot on his back and shoved hard. He went down on his face, sprawling in the grass. Angry, he tried to rise again as she reached for a fallen limb several inches thick and a yard long.

Dan reined up, fascinated.

As the attacker started to get up, she reared back with the limb and then swung hard. The wood struck him over his shoulders so hard and fast that he lost his balance. He fell, wildly grabbing the air and crashing into the rushing water. He flailed angrily in the current, but managed to grab the brush along the bank.

The man with the six-gun grinned.

The woman turned with the limb in

her hand, walking over to him as he kept her escort on his knees.

'Get away from him,' she said.

The grinning man holstered his six-gun and grabbed at the limb, pulling her toward him. She released the limb enough to let him fall back a step. Then she shoved hard, the branch hitting him in the gut. He gasped and fell backward over the kneeling man.

The kneeling escort stood up, his pink face darkly flushed. He moved to stand with the young woman, who took his arm. The fallen man got to his feet, his beady eyes flashing, his fat mouth twisted as he drew his six-gun.

'Now you're in for it.' His voice was coarse and nasty.

At that moment, Dan intervened. It had been many years since he had been able to smile from the heart, but right now, he was grinning. It felt so strange to smile. The fat-lipped man backed away, staring up at Dan's badge and slowly holstering his gun.

'We were just funnin', Marshal,' he snarled.

From the river, the other man dragged himself onto the bank, sputtering and soaked. He had lost his hat.

Dan turned in the saddle to look down at the woman. She was in her early twenties, and had the prettiest eyes he had ever seen — dark blue like a mountain lake. She had a small nose, delicate lips, and high cheekbones, and her skin was the color of peaches. The green dress with velvet trim, torn at the sleeve, snugged her shapely form. And the golden hair that spilled about her shoulders was gleaming in the sunlight. She was a sight to behold.

'Listen, Marshal,' the soaked man said as he staggered up, 'we were just foolin' around. I'm Kirk Seton, and this here's my friend Char Olson. Maybe you heard of him.'

Dan studied him. So this was one of Giles Seton's sons. Seton had tried to run the valley twelve years ago. Dan would never forget how his father had

8

stood up to Seton's bullying and land-grabbing more than once.

Seton had a ruddy face with a small red mustache, red-brown hair, a jutting chin, and chunky cheekbones. In his mid-thirties, he was old enough to have been on the raid. Stocky and well-muscled in a red wool shirt, he would be dangerous in a fistfight. The six-gun at his side rested in a cut-down holster.

'Be on your way,' Dan said.

Seton, running his hand over his wet hair, turned to glare at the woman and her companion. 'This ain't finished, college boy.' Then he started for his horse, Olson following.

Dan sat watching them. Olson was dangling his hands by his side. As they neared their horses, Seton wiped his head again, using his bandanna to dry his face. Seton wasn't going to draw, Dan decided, but Olson was aching for it.

The two men muttered to each other as they mounted. Then Seton rode forward, reining up to look Dan straight in the eye.

'So why are you here, Marshal?'

'I'm lookin' for a man.'

'Anyone I know?'

'Maybe.'

When it was obvious they would learn no more, the two men turned and rode up the bank. Olson glanced back over his shoulder with menace. Dan knew he might have to kill that man one day.

When the riders were gone, Dan twisted in the saddle to look at the young couple. The young man was plenty embarrassed. His pink face turned several shades of color as the woman knelt to gather up the picnic.

'My name's Josh Hartley, Marshal. This lady is Virginia Creighton. Her uncle owns the newspaper in Rawhide.'

Dan knew the Hartleys had been neutral twelve years ago, refusing to come to the meetings at his father's ranch. He vaguely recalled that their spread was west of town and south of the river, opposite the Setons.

The girl stood up slowly, the basket dangling from her small, slender hands. It was obvious she was badly shaken. Her bravado was waning now that the danger was gone.

She looked up at him, squinting in the sunlight. 'They'd been drinking. We're glad you came, Marshal.'

'Maybe you'd better ride with us,' Josh said. 'If you're going to Rawhide.'

Dan nodded and silently watched as Josh assisted Virginia into the buggy. He felt sorry for the young man, so out of place on the frontier. The gray horse in the harness lifted its head as Josh took the reins and turned it up the slope. The big skinny wheels wobbled and jumped until they were on the trail that followed the river westward.

Riding near them on Virginia's side, Dan watched the way her flaxen hair blew in the wind. She cast quick glances at him and often smiled. She was a breath of fresh air on his bitter trail.

As they rode across the rolling hills in sight of distant herds, Dan gazed at the far-off mountains circling the valley. Wild River was fed by melting snow and little creeks that hurried down from those high reaches. The grass was tall and green and sweet-smelling, with little yellow and blue flowers sprinkled along their path.

Somewhere out there was Shanks's place, but, according to his letter, the old man had moved into town. The letter was six months old when it reached Dan in Denver. In it, Shanks had promised the truth about the death of Dan's family. Shanks had been too afraid to write the names of the culprits in his letter, and Dan's imagination had been going crazy ever since.

Dan was glad to finally see Rawhide in the distance. But the town was not the little cluster of buildings that he remembered. It was a dozen times bigger, sprawling south to north along the river, where a high wooden bridge had replaced the old ferry. A church and schoolhouse rested on a far hill west of town, near the big white hotel.

The memory of wagon rides to town deepened his thoughts. Again, he was that fifteen-year-old boy, holding his sister Ann in his arms in the smoke-filled cellar, feeling her life fade away as he cried and begged her to live. He was that same boy, who, hours later, choking and gasping for air, crawled through the burned-out cellar door at the back of the house just before the floor collapsed.

He had stumbled through the ashes to turn and look at the ruins of the ranch house. Nothing was left. The cattle and horses had run off, leaving a silence shaken only by the wind.

Shattered and weak from loss of blood, he half-crawled to the nearby ranch of Will Shanks. The kindly man took him in, and knifed out the bullet from his shoulder. Shanks, fearful for Dan's life, let the world believe the entire Cassidy family had died in the fire. Then Shanks had made discreet inquiries for him, but with no success.

'It's no use, Dan,' he had said. 'No one admits to knowin' anything. You ain't never gonna find out if it was the Setons or anyone else, but they wanted Cassidy grass, that's for sure. And your pa was the only one who could organize the small ranchers. If the killers knowed you was still alive, they'd come after you so folks wouldn't rally around you. I got me a cousin down in Texas where you can be safe.'

Texas became Dan's new home, though he never forgot the injustice of the unsolved murders. At Shanks's insistence, he changed his last name from Cassidy to Casey.

In Texas, Shanks's cousin, a gunman with a shady reputation, taught Dan how to make a gun leap into his hand.

'You got the knack,' the gunman assured him when Dan was only seventeen. 'I sure wouldn't want to come against you.'

Dan knew that someday he would

return to this valley, but he wanted to come back with power instead of blind, hopeless rage. That power was the badge on his black leather vest, earned after hours of poring over law books with a judge as his teacher. It had taken years to obtain a federal badge, and it would take him right where he wanted to be.

But ever since he had received Shanks's letter, all he could think of was the vengeance that had smoldered in his gut for twelve years. He prayed he would have the strength to keep himself from doing anything but arresting the killers.

Glancing at the pretty young woman in the buggy, he thought of how he had not taken time for warmth or romance. A woman like this would bring sunshine to a man's world.

He thought of his mother's sweet smile, and the way she smelled of soap as she wrapped her plump arms around him, holding him and kissing him as he struggled.

'Ma, I'm fifteen years old,' he had protested.

She always laughed, her pretty face rosy in the sunlight. He looked at his father, big and husky, cutting the timber they had hauled from the mountains. His father worked hard for the spread and never rested. He was full of laughter, but he had his serious moments.

'Son, when you grow up, remember there's more to bein' a man than wearin' a gun or fightin'. You got to think, Dan. You got to know where you're goin', and you got to plan.'

Others had listened to his father. The secret meetings of the small ranchers at the Cassidy house had brought men who had heeded his father's advice and counsel. Plans had been brewing for a fight against the night raiders who were trying to run them out of the valley.

Dan swallowed hard at his memories, for he never really had accepted his loss. Shutting it away had been his only means of bearing the pain. He prayed for the day the truth would be known.

Dan rode around the buggy, glancing at Virginia again as he tipped his hat, then rode on ahead. It was near twilight and getting colder. As he entered the busy street, he saw men heading for the saloons. Other men and women turned toward home, children tagging along behind, dogs barking. Two wagons were being loaded at the general store. Mules were packed down by the livery, a reminder there was a silver camp in the mountains at the head of Wild River.

Dan gazed about as he rode. A pretty young woman in front of the mercantile paused to look at him. She was wearing a pink dress and her red hair was done up in tight curls. She gazed at him with interest, then smiled and turned away.

He reined up in front of the newspaper office. Inside, a lamp was already burning. He could see a man at a desk, and figured the editor would know how to find Shanks.

Dan dismounted and left his stallion at the rail. At the door, he paused to watch the buggy approach in the twilight.

Josh Hartley pulled the gray to a halt near the railing. He sprang down to help Virginia step to the ground, handing her the basket. He bowed as he kissed her hand, then he climbed back into the buggy and drove away, his shoulders hunched in his continued embarrassment.

Virginia turned slowly to look at Dan, then came over to join him. She smiled as she spoke.

'That was Laura Seton across the street.'

'I didn't notice.'

She laughed, her eyes twinkling, then turned to the door. 'My uncle is Sid Creighton, the editor. Please come in.'

She knocked. The man peered through the dirty window. When he saw them, he quickly unbarred the door and allowed them to enter, then set the bar in place once more. He pulled down the shades.

The room was square, its walls lined

with tables and trays of type separated in tiny dividers. A hand-run press stood in the center of the room. There was newsprint all over the floor in stacks. Ink was everywhere, including all over the man's white shirt and wrinkled face.

Creighton was in his late sixties, graying and stooped. He wore spectacles and had a pointed chin. He wiped his hands on his shirt, spreading more black streaks.

'I'm Marshal Dan Casey, Mr. Creighton.'

Squinting at Dan, Creighton beckoned to the chairs around his desk. Dan clumsily stepped aside as Virginia sat down. He seated himself in the wooden chair a few feet from her and gazed at the editor, who was too busy looking at his niece.

'Virginia, you look flushed. And your sleeve is torn. Everything all right?'

'Of course, Uncle Sid. Josh and I had our picnic, but we had visitors. Kirk Seton and Char Olson.'

'What happened?'

'Nothing much. They had been drinking. Kirk was making trouble, but the marshal came along and scared them away.'

'If one of them put his hands on you — '

Dan smiled. 'I have a feeling she can take care of herself.'

Creighton chuckled. 'You're right about that. Before we came here three years ago, we'd already been kicked out of a few places. Once we had to shoot our way out. But we always managed to bring the press.'

Virginia nodded. 'So far, we haven't been kicked out of Rawhide.'

'If my editorials were getting anywhere, I'd have been burned out or shot by now.'

She turned to Dan. 'My uncle wants the valley cleaned up. He writes some powerful words, but he doesn't know who to put in jail.'

Creighton nodded. 'I'm not sure who's responsible for all the killin' and thievin' that's been goin' on, but I know who has the most to gain. The more ranchers and settlers that move on, the more the Setons and Hartleys can spread out.'

'Now Uncle Sid, don't get your heart to racing.'

'My niece reads a lot of books, you know. Even medical books. All that instead of gettin' herself a husband. Why, I wouldn't even object to Josh Hartley, since he's been back East so long and hasn't been sullied by his family. And Karl Seton — he runs the bank and is clean and a real gentleman, not anything like his brother Kirk. But no, she's got to spend her time readin'.'

Dan looked from one to the other. He saw the kind of affection and companionship he had not known since he was fifteen. He was envious.

'There are other troublemakers in town, Marshal,' the editor continued. 'Miners come through in a hurry, by stage or wagon or on mules, headin' upriver on the north side to Wild River Camp. And when they come back through, they're either spendin' all their earnings at the gambling hall or they're broke and stealin'.'

'Where's your sheriff?'

Creighton shook his head. 'We had Sheriff Denson, but he was shot down about five months ago. His wife came out from Tennessee a few weeks ago, only to find he was dead. Now no one wants the job, and this town sure ain't electing a Seton or a Hartley. Jail's boarded up. Maybe we can clean it up for you to use while you're here. I mean, I hope you're staying.'

Dan tried to look calm as he spoke. 'When I was going through the files on this town, I found an old letter from a man named Shanks, written about twelve years ago. It mentioned the Cassidy murders. You know where I can find him?'

The editor stared at him. 'Shanks? Why, he was shot down about six months ago, a few weeks afore the sheriff. They found him in an alley. He's buried out in the church cemetery.'

Dan felt shock waves running through him. Sweat came to his face. The letter in his pocket burned through his clothes and seared his flesh, but it was useless now. His witness was dead.

He cleared his throat. 'What do you know about Giles Seton and John Hartley?'

'Well, Hartley died off. His ticker, I guess. His boys mostly run things.'

'And Seton?'

'Giles is gettin' on, and he hardly comes to town. But his sons are kickin' up a lot of the trouble, I suspect. Them and the Hartley boys. Ridin' roughshod over everyone.'

Virginia frowned. 'No one feels safe.'

Her uncle leaned back, arms folded. 'I'm even suspicious of Tex Barker over at the gamblin' hall. He always seems to have his hand in something.'

'Uncle Sid thinks they're all waiting on the railroad.'

Creighton nodded. 'The Denver & Rio Grande Railroad has been sniffing around. There's a good chance they'll cut through here to get business from the mines.'

Dan nodded, then looked around the cluttered shop. 'Looks like a lot of work in here.'

'Virginia's my printer's devil when I let her,' Creighton said, grinning. 'But I make her wear gloves.'

'I told him that I want one of those fancy typing machines,' Virginia said. 'Remington took a Sholes & Glidden machine and made it better. We saw one in St. Louis.'

'Don't need no machines,' Creighton stated. 'I think as I set type. I know what I want to say. Just get me some ready-print and I'll put in my editorial.'

'Ready-print?' Dan asked.

Creighton leaned over and picked up sheets that had news from the East printed on one side but nothing on the other, giving the frontier paper a chance to add its own stories. The printed side was covered with advertisements.

Dan stood up slowly. 'Well, I have to take care of my horse.'

'Stable's up by the river.'

'I'll show the marshal where to go,' Virginia said. 'And maybe he could spend the night with us.'

'Good idea. How about it, Marshal? You come back here after you take care of your horse. We got lots of extra room.'

Dan hesitated. 'I'd just be making you a target.'

'We already are, son. They just shot an editor up in Denver. We could use a little protection.'

Virginia followed Dan outside into the darkness, closing the door behind her. Light spilled from the buildings, caressing her face and glistening in her eyes. New feelings stirred within him, so unexpected he didn't know what to do with them.

'I never had a chance to thank you, Marshal.'

'Dan.'

'I went too far, you know. Kirk was pretty angry. If you hadn't ridden up, I don't know what would have happened.

But strange as it might seem, Kirk has proposed marriage several times. So has Karl Seton. And Josh Hartley.'

'And a dozen others?'

She smiled at the compliment. 'Maybe.'

'Well, I'd forget about Kirk.'

'He and that man Olson had been drinking, or I wouldn't have gotten away with what I did. But I'll never forgive them for humiliating Josh. He doesn't even wear a gun.'

'Did you and your uncle really shoot your way out of a town?'

She laughed. 'Yes, over in Kansas. Actually, we were leaving, and the men escorting us started shooting to scare our horses. We shot back, but we just shot up in the air. But it made them turn back.'

'Still, it was risky.'

'Like most editors, my uncle's very outspoken. Back in Virginia, when I was small, he was for the Union in the wrong town. They nearly hanged him. But I held on and cried, and they took

pity. But they ran us out. We were
invited to leave again, up near St. Louis
and then in Kansas. We came here
because we hoped the war would be
behind us. Instead, we found a different
kind of war.'

'Is he your only kin?'

'Yes, my father died in the war. My
mother died when I was born. That's
why I keep reading Doc's books. And I
help him sometimes. When I have
children, I want to know how to save
myself and them.'

Dan gazed at her for a long moment,
admiring her intelligence. Then he
walked to the rail in the moonlight. His
stallion nosed him and tossed its head.
Virginia came to stand at Dan's side,
the breeze catching her scent of roses.

She pointed down the street. 'That
fourth building on your left is the jail,
near the smithy. The livery's on your
right, way over by the river. You can
leave your gear with us. We'll wait for
you.'

He removed his saddlebags, bedroll,

and rifle, which he set over by the door of the newspaper office.

He mounted his horse, and leaned on the pommel to look down at her. She was different from his mother in appearance, but she had the same gentle warmth, the same pretty smile. He basked in the glow of her, knowing she was any man's dream. But he had no heart left.

'Be careful,' she said.

'*Be careful,*' his mother had said. '*You're going to fall in the creek. Then what will I do, Danny? I won't have a little boy to hug.*'

Dan straightened, a lump in his throat. He had never allowed anyone to call him Danny since the murders. It would be too painful.

Glancing away from Virginia, he touched the edge of his hat in a gentlemanly way and rode past the dark jail on his left. It was cold, and the chill cut under his coat. Stars gleamed overhead like diamonds on a black blanket.

The town consisted of an express office with a stage depot and one large bank. It also had two cafés, a bakery, a laundry, several saloons, a gambling hall on his right, two barbers, a billiard parlor, two hardware stores, a boot shop, and a small livery across from the large one. There was also an undertaker and a doctor, the latter with his office above a store.

Dan stabled his stallion at the larger livery and rubbed him down. Then he walked back down the street. He heard laughter and music from the saloons, where smoke curled out into the night. It was cold and dark, except for the lights from the windows.

Somewhere in this town or out in the valley, the men who had killed his family were as free as the buzzards. His witness was dead, and his badge made him a target. He had no choice but to move slowly.

As he passed the gambling hall, he glanced through the smoked windows at the fancy decor and the busy tables. Miners, cowmen, and drifters were enjoying every moment of their chances. He remembered what Creighton had said about the suspicious owner, Tex Barker.

Grimly, he headed for the newspaper office.

Inside, Virginia was chattering to her uncle while they waited for Dan.

'Uncle Sid, what do you think of the marshal?'

'He's a mighty hard man.'

'I'd like to soften him up.'

He gazed at her curiously. 'You got all these fellas in town chasin' you. Why the marshal?'

'I don't know. He's so much more than that badge, and I'd like to find out why.'

'From what I heard of Dan Casey, he's more of a gunfighter than a lawman. Some say he was an outlaw afore he put on a badge.'

'There are stories about everyone, Uncle Sid. I'm sure they tell some fine tales about you.'

'And most of 'em true, you can bet on it.'

She laughed, reaching over to tickle his chin.

Suddenly, they heard a shot.

2

Hearing the shot, Dan hurried back along the boardwalk in the darkness. Another shot rang out from the gambling hall on the right side of the street. He paused just outside the swinging doors and looked into the plush palace, with its green felt-covered tables and fancy hanging lanterns. A walnut bar to the right had huge decorated mirrors behind it, next to a series of paintings. A piano in the corner was silent.

The crowd inside had fallen away from the center of the room, where two men remained at a table. The dealer, in a white shirt and red vest pulled tight over his big belly, was sweating profusely. Blood trickled from both his ear lobes.

A short man in an ill-fitting, store-bought suit stood opposite him, his back to Dan. He had a gun aimed at the dealer's middle.

'This time, dead center,' the man snarled.

'Hold it,' Dan said.

Slowly, the man turned. He was scrawny, with a pointed chin. He leveled his six-gun at Dan as he spoke insolently.

'Get out of here, Marshal. This is between me and them. I come back with a bag full of gold and these coyotes took near all of it away from me. I aim to get it back.'

'Put your gun down.'

'Back off, Marshal.'

Dan started slowly toward him. The man drew back the hammer with his other hand. He raised his gun straight at Dan's face, his finger on the trigger.

'Too bad, Marshal. Say your prayers.'

As the man squeezed the trigger, Dan jumped aside and drew his gun, his weapon leaping into his hand the way he had been trained day after day, night after night, in Texas. They fired at the same time, both shots ringing like one loud cannon.

The man staggered forward under the force of the bullet in his heart. He stared at Dan as he fired again, missing. He fell to his knees, then rolled over on his side.

'Nice shot, Marshal.'

The voice was suave and cultured. Dan turned slowly to face a man in his forties who looked for all the world like a riverboat gambler. Coming through the swinging doors, he wore a fancy little tie, a red vest, and a pin-striped suit, his six-gun strapped under a long coat. His face was thin and colorful. He had shiny dark eyes to match his slick hair and trim handlebar mustache. But the smile on his lips seemed genuine.

There was something familiar about his lazy walk, and Dan wondered if he knew him from somewhere. Even his voice had a tone he remembered.

'I'm Tex Barker. This is my place.'

'Did you cheat that man?'

'Hey,' the dealer cut in, 'I was

handlin' them cards fair and square. That fella just didn't know when to quit.'

'That's right, Marshal,' an onlooker said.

Tex was still smiling. 'Come on, Marshal, I'll buy you a drink.'

Dan walked with him to the bar, ordered coffee, and leaned on the shiny wood as he looked around the room, which had returned to normal. Cards were dealt, men were smoking, drinking, and arguing. There was laughter.

'Big crowd,' Dan said.

'Well, it's Saturday night.' Tex leaned over the bar. 'You're the first federal law ever showed up around here. Some people get a little nervous when they see that badge.'

'You one of them?'

Tex smiled lazily. 'Maybe.'

'Why didn't your men take care of that guy before he started shooting?'

'I don't know, but that was some trick, drawing on a man with a gun in his hand.'

'But you figure you could have done as well.'

'That's right, Marshal.'

'I don't suppose there are any handbills out on you.'

'Not in Colorado.'

Dan studied him. As slick as the man appeared, he couldn't help but like him. There was something truthful about his attitude — there was nothing secretly sinister behind his easy smile. Dan still couldn't figure out why he seemed familiar, but whoever the man was, he had nothing to hide.

'Thanks for the coffee.'

'Any time, Marshal.'

Dan walked through the crowd, feeling men watching him. Outside, he breathed the fresh cold air and headed for the jail. Two doors down and on the other side, a light still burned in the doctor's office above the general store.

As he crossed the street, a shot rang out, singing by his right ear. He dived for cover behind a wagon. Another bullet thudded into the boards near his head. It came from an alley next to the gambling hall.

He could hear someone running away. He darted around the wagon, sweat on his face, and raced back across the street, six-gun in hand. He reached the alley just as he heard hoofbeats beyond the gambling hall.

He ran into the open and saw nothing but darkness. He thought of Kirk Seton and Char Olson, or maybe a friend of the man he had just killed in the hall.

As he returned to the street, he saw Tex Barker emerge from the hall with his six-gun in hand. The gambler stood in the pale light of the window and holstered his weapon as Dan approached.

'Marshal, that badge is a real target.' He leaned on a post supporting the roof. 'You know, I have me a feelin' you're not just passin' through. I know most everything that goes on around here. Maybe I can help you out.'

Dan studied him in the pale light. He

gave him a closer look.

'Where are you from, Tex?'

'New Orleans, thereabouts. Been here five years now.'

'You seem to be doin' pretty well for yourself. That ring looks like a diamond. So does that stickpin.'

'Right you are, Marshal. I've even been courtin' Laura Seton. I have manners. She likes that.'

Dan shrugged. 'I ain't here for Laura Seton.'

'Then why are you here?'

'One reason has to do with some murders twelve years ago.'

Tex straightened, his eyes gleaming. 'Ah, the Cassidy family. I heard about that. Well, all you have to do is go out and see the cattle grazin' there. I think you'll find they're all wearing Seton's brand. He even bought the ranch when it was sold at public auction for taxes. Beat the Hartleys out of it.'

Dan remained silent, so the gambler went back inside. Slowly, Dan turned down the street, heading back to the newspaper office, where a lamp still burned. He joined Creighton and filled him in on the gunshots, then waited as the editor closed up and led him out the back way.

They walked up a slope to a rambling white house with a circling porch. Inside the front room, warmth glowed from the huge stone hearth. The place was neatly furnished and comfortable.

'My niece has gone to bed,' Creighton said. 'She was plumb worn out, but she said you'd better stay for breakfast.'

Creighton offered him supper and coffee. After he ate, Dan went up to a room at the top of the stairs. He closed the door and sat on the bed as he surveyed the small but neat room. His saddlebags, bedroll, and Winchester lay on the bed. A pitcher of water and a bowl stood on the chest of drawers, next to a towel.

He lay back in the pale light of the lamp and took out the letter, unfolding the worn pages to read Shanks's scribbled but legible handwriting:

Dan, I know who done it. I learned it from one of the killers hisself. He was drunk, and I was listening. You'd better get here while you got me alive. I'm too afraid to write down the names. Look for me in town. I sold my place to Seton 'cause I was getting too old. This letter's goin' to Texas, and I sure hope it follows you if you ain't there.

One more thing, Dan. I sure been proud of you for takin' the straight and narrow.

It was signed by Shanks six months ago, about the time he was killed. Someone must have figured he knew too much. Folding it, Dan closed his eyes to stop the tears. So close to justice, yet all he had was a letter with no live witness. But if he could find Shanks's killers, he might learn the rest.

He spent a miserable night, but in the morning, he was treated to Virginia's smiling face and terrific cooking. The biscuits were hot and fluffy, and the eggs and bacon smelled so good, he could taste them before they hit his mouth.

Creighton leaned back in his chair as she cleared the dishes. 'Listen, it's Sunday. We was hopin' you'd go on to church with us. Afterward, we can help you clean up the jail.'

Dan could think of no graceful way out, but he remembered his family's prayers. Maybe now was the time to seek guidance.

The small church on the hill should have had some hundred or more people crowded inside. Instead, only about forty attended. Most were merchants and their families.

Laura Seton sat in a nearby pew, casting friendly glances at Dan. Her red hair and gray-blue eyes made her unusual and fetching. She wore a shiny blue dress and a lot of white lace.

Dan looked at Virginia, who was seated at his side. She was lovely in a different way, more soft and gentle. Her large, dark blue eyes were enough to drown a man. Her long golden hair was drawn back from her face, tumbling in soft waves down her back.

Outside in the sunlight after the services, people expressed their thanks to Dan for coming to town. Men came to shake his hand, including a portly merchant named John Beeker, who told Dan he'd had some law training.

'I've been trying to buy the newspaper from Creighton here,' Beeker added, 'but he won't sell. And it's a shame. I could do a lot of good in this town.'

Laura approached, but the man with her caught her arm, slowing her. He had a ruddy face and chunky cheekbones under a pretentious top hat.

'Marshal, I'm Karl Seton,' he said, introducing himself. 'I run the bank in town. May I present my sister, Laura Seton?'

'Dan Casey.'

'Marshal,' Laura said, moving closer, 'it must be terribly exciting in Denver. I would love to see the opera there. We had a theater group here, but it left.'

Virginia stiffened. 'I don't think the marshal has time for opera.'

'Matter of fact,' Dan said, 'I have seen one. It was pretty noisy, but I liked it.'

Miffed, Virginia turned away and started downhill with her uncle, Karl at her heels.

Dan and Laura were left alone. He felt uncomfortable, tipped his hat, and started to turn away.

'Marshal, wait.'

He paused, and she came a little closer as she opened her parasol. 'Have you seen the falls, Marshal?'

He swallowed hard, shaking his head. But a memory swept over him. His father had taken him upriver to see the great falls by way of the Hartleys' ranch and a long narrow canyon. They had passed through an area of free grass on both sides of the shallow river, where Seton and Hartley cattle often mingled.

It had been a thrilling adventure,

riding his own pony and following the white water, hearing the roar of the falls. The noise grew ever louder as they neared. Then they had come over a rise, and they saw the majesty of it.

Laura's soft voice was persistent.

'Perhaps you'd like to see the falls on a picnic. Shall we say tomorrow?'

He shrugged, feeling awkward. 'I'm sorry, I can't. But that's a right nice offer. Maybe another day.'

'Another day then,' she said, taking his arm.

Dan's face was hot as he walked down the hill with her. She chatted about people and things, but he wasn't listening.

At the bottom of the slope, Laura released his arm and turned to gaze up at him, her eyes twinkling. 'I'm staying in town with my brother. That big white house over there on that far hill, toward the river.'

Karl came back to them and took his sister's arm, bidding Dan good day. Laura smiled at him over her shoulder.

Relieved, Dan joined Virginia, who was still miffed, and her uncle. The three of them walked into the quiet main street.

There was a peaceful stillness, with no wind, no loud noises from the saloon or gambling hall, no creaky wagons moving.

Suddenly, a crude voice rang out. 'Marshal, you'd better turn around.'

3

In the middle of the dusty street stood the biggest man that Dan had ever seen. He was over seven feet tall, and had huge shoulders too wide for any doorway. The size of his head was almost too small, and his black beard was like a bush covering his lower face and all of his neck. From his clothes, it was obvious he was a miner, and he wasn't wearing a side arm. He took a clumsy step forward.

'Marshal, you shot down my little brother last night. I'm gonna break your neck.'

Even the man's voice was big. Dan stood with his breath caught in his chest as he surveyed his new opponent. He tried to look calm and unruffled.

'Your brother was about to kill a man when I stepped in. Then he turned his gun on me. I had to shoot back.'

'You killed my little brother. That's all I know.'

'What's your name?'

'Hoot Hammer. And that's enough talk.'

The giant advanced slowly, long arms swinging. The man looked strong enough to break a wagon in half, not to mention Dan.

Virginia tugged at Dan's arm. 'Please, don't fight him.'

Dan shook off her fingers. Creighton took her arm and led her to where the church crowd had begun to gather at the foot of the hill. The street was empty, but men came out on the boardwalks to watch. One of them was Tex Barker, who seemed plenty amused.

Hammer was only a few yards from Dan and approaching like a waddling grizzly. Dan swallowed hard. He could pull his six-gun and order the man back, but he knew it wouldn't stop Hammer. He'd have to kill him, and Dan didn't want to do that. This man

47

was grieving for his little brother.

Dan backed slowly toward the hitching rail. He noticed the crossbar was loose, so he grabbed it and tried to jerk it free. But it was stuck on one end. He pushed back his hat and looked in every direction. There was nothing handy for him to use.

A spring wagon stood nearby with a pitchfork leaning from the empty bed, but he didn't want to kill this man. The team of horses was alert, one pawing the ground near the big watering trough in front of the smithy. Behind the trough was a large stack of tin buckets and iron pans.

As Hammer closed in, Dan took a step aside and circled him. They moved farther into the dusty street. Dan moistened his dry lips.

Suddenly, the man charged like a locomotive.

Dan sidestepped and dug his fist into the big middle. The man's stomach was as hard as a rock, nearly breaking Dan's hand. Dan swallowed his silent yell and ducked as Hammer charged again.

Big hands swept by Dan's head like a hurricane. Dan dodged the next rush and backed over to the wagon. The giant came roaring at him, hands reaching. Dan jumped behind the wagon near the trough. Hammer came around the wagon with a roar. Dan tripped as he moved backward and fell on the boardwalk.

Hammer was on him like a building caving in, three hundred pounds of muscle dropping on him even as he rolled to the side. Big knees just missed Dan's middle. He tried to get up, but Hammer grabbed him by one arm and lifted him in the air like a toy.

He threw Dan into the stacks of tin buckets and iron pots. Crashing into the stacks, Dan fell like a rag doll, trying to prevent injury. He scrambled to his feet, an iron pan in each hand, just as Hammer put his huge arms around Dan's waist and lifted him in the air.

Dan crashed the two iron skillets

together against both of the man's ears. Eyes glazed, Hammer faltered but kept crushing Dan like a vise. Dan slammed the skillets again against the man's ears, so hard he thought the man's eyes rolled.

Stunned, Hammer let Dan fall back into the stacks. Holding his ears in his big hands, the giant lost his balance and fell backward into the big watering trough near the smithy. But it wasn't big enough for him. He split the trough as he landed, the sides falling out with a flood of water.

Hammer was still dazed as Dan rolled him out of the trough and onto his face. As Hammer finally got on his knees, he was staring into Dan's six-gun. The barrel was inches from his nose.

'Mr. Creighton,' Dan called, 'I'd appreciate it if you'd open the jail.'

Not convinced the giant couldn't break the bars with one hand, Dan marched the dizzy Hammer to the jail. Creighton led the way, and other men came to help. With an iron bar, they knocked the boards from the front door and windows. Several men hurried inside to locate the keys and open the larger of the two cells in the back room.

Only when Hammer was in the locked cell, still shaking his head, and the door to the back was closed on the cells, did the other men start to laugh.

Dan sat down at the dusty desk, his body aching. The hard wooden chair with swivels underneath hurt his every move. The men left, but Creighton remained, and Virginia cautiously came inside, making sure it was safe.

'I hope you didn't hurt that man,' Virginia said.

Dan looked at her smile, then had to laugh. It felt mighty strange to feel mirth bubbling out.

'He'll have a bad headache,' he said.

Creighton grinned and looked around the office. 'Yeah, I imagine his ears are still ringing. Say, this place sure is dirty.'

'We'll come back later and help,' Virginia said.

They left Dan to his aching body. He leaned back in the chair. Suddenly, the jail shook like the earth was moving under it. The walls rattled. The floor seemed to roll. Dan jumped to his feet, six-gun in hand, and opened the back door, heading down the short hallway to the cells.

Hammer had a bar in each hand and was shaking the cell fiercely. Dan swallowed, not convinced the man couldn't break it all down. But he approached casually, holstering his gun and keeping out of reach.

'Hammer, you'd better listen to me. I shot your brother to save the dealer and my own life. You got a problem with that?'

Hammer shook the bars some more, his eyes wild.

'Marshal, I gotta do somethin'. He was my only brother. Now I got nobody and I gotta kill somebody.'

The big voice faded out. Hammer

stopped shaking the bars and leaned his head against them. Tears filled his beady eyes and trickled down into his greasy, matted beard.

'Hammer, there's nothing you can do.'

'That Tex Barker, he took his money. I know them tables are crooked. I warned my brother. Look out for the sirens, I said. Look out for the cards.'

'You don't know they're crooked. Why don't you go back to your mine?'

'It was a glory hole, lots of gold nuggets, but it played out. I sent my little brother here to bank the gold, but he didn't go to the bank. This is a dirty town, Marshal. Now I got nothin'.'

'Then go on home.'

'What home? All we had was our old grandpa back East, and he had no place for us.'

'Then get a job on one of the ranches.'

'I ride a big mule, Marshal. It ain't easy herdin' cows with a big, clubfooted mule. I can't ride no horse they got around here.'

'You could work for the railroad, out in the flats.'

'Yeah, maybe I'll do that.'

Dan started to turn away, then stopped. Slowly, he turned and looked at the man in the cell.

'I could use a deputy while I'm here. Keep the place clean. Act as a jailer. Watch my back in the street. Can you shoot?'

Hammer wiped the tears from his eyes and blinked at Dan. 'I can use a rifle and a shotgun.'

'You wanted anywhere?'

'No, I ain't.'

'Can you make coffee?'

The big man, still stunned, nodded. Dan went back for the keys, telling himself he was crazy. But he needed someone to watch his back. He had no time to find some other deputy.

Trying to be nonchalant, he unlocked the cell, then turned back toward the front office. He felt cold all over, as if the devil was about to grab him from behind. The floor shook a little with the big man's steps.

Dan made it to his desk and sat down, turning to look at Hammer. 'There's a pot and some coffee next to the stove in the corner.'

'Marshal, you're a bigger man than you look.'

With that, Hammer turned and waddled over to the iron stove. He stuffed it with wood and started a fire. Then he filled the pot with water from a pitcher and set it on top.

Dan busied himself with the posters on the wall and in the desk. The sheriff had not kept any kind of log, unless it had been stolen. When the scent of coffee began to waft into the air, he looked up, and Hammer handed him a cup. It tasted good.

'I can cook too, Marshal.'

Just then the door opened and Virginia came hurrying in. She wore a bandanna over her hair and some kind of coverall apron. A broom was in one hand, and a mop in the other.

She came to a halt in the middle of the room and stared up at Hammer, nearly fainting with fright. Then she saw Dan's calm smile and how Hammer backed away from her.

'My new deputy,' Dan said. 'Hoot Hammer.'

'What?'

'My new deputy.'

Creighton entered at Dan's last words. He was carrying Dan's saddle-bags, bedroll, and Winchester. He stared at the giant, who sat down on the bench by the stove.

'Well, you sure picked a good one,' Creighton said. 'Won't no one be giving you any trouble while he's around.'

Virginia had recovered. 'You have to leave, Dan. I can't clean up with you here. And take Mr. Hammer with you.'

Dan shrugged. 'I got to go through these papers.'

'Later,' she said.

Creighton laughed. 'There's no use arguing with a woman, Dan. Haven't you ever learned that? Come on, I'll buy you and your new deputy a cup of coffee.'

When the three men had filed out into the street, Virginia set about cleaning the jail. She finished her work and stood about surveying the place. The front windows were clean and shining. The curtains were still dirty, however. Dragging a chair over, she stood on it and examined the rotting fabric. She gave a hard jerk, lost her balance, and fell backward from the chair with a gasp.

Suddenly, big arms caught her, and her head rolled back against a shoulder. She cried out and looked up, but it wasn't Hammer. It was Dan.

She lay in his grasp, her bandanna dragged back from her golden hair. His arms were around her waist and under her dangling legs. His hat had fallen back from his wavy brown hair.

Dan couldn't believe he was holding a beautiful woman in his arms. She looked breathless, one arm caught against his chest, the other still holding a piece of rotted curtain. Her dark blue eyes were round with surprise.

There was nothing else a man could do.

He bent his head and kissed her. She relaxed in his arms, responding softly. His heart swelled in his chest. It was a joyous, wondrous moment.

Both were fighting for breath as he drew back. He gazed at her surprise and swallowed hard. Then he abruptly set her on her feet and backed away as if she were dangerous. She tried to appear ruffled and angry.

'Dan Casey, you took advantage of me.'

He grinned. 'I'm sorry I did. I didn't know you were so dirty.'

She fought back a smile. 'What's more, those curtains are stuck up there. I'll make you some more, but you have to take that rod down.'

'I'll hold you while you get back up there,' he offered slyly.

'You'll do no such thing.'

'I don't want you to fall.'

Before she could answer, a woman appeared in the doorway. It was Laura Seton, curious and smiling.

'Why, Miss Creighton, do you work here?'

'I'm just a volunteer.'

Dan bent over to pick up his hat, but he knew that Laura sensed more was going on here than a cleaning job. He nodded to her and went back to his desk.

'Were you just leaving, Miss Creighton?' Laura asked.

'Yes, but I'm coming right back.'

Virginia picked up the broom and mop, shoved the bucket she had used against the wall, then hurried out into the fading sunlight.

Laura waited a long moment, then came over to Dan, who was shuffling papers. 'Marshal, I came to invite you to supper.'

'You're too late,' Virginia said from the doorway. 'He's already coming to our house.'

The two women gazed at each other, looking for weakness. Then Virginia spun on her heel and left. The door remained open. Laura smiled and drew herself up.

'I'm here because you are invited to my brother Karl's for supper, any night you choose. We're both curious about you.'

'And I'm curious about the Setons. Your father ever come into town?'

'Not very often.'

'I'd like to ride out and see him.'

'Karl and I would be glad to go with you. You'll find my father is really a wonderful man. But what about our picnic?'

He shrugged. 'Right now, I just want to find out what's going on around here.'

'Well, you won't learn anything from Miss Creighton. They've only been here three years. And her uncle's newspaper is full of foolishness.'

Dan shuffled some more papers. She was making him nervous, the way she was standing so close.

Just then, a man appeared in the doorway. It was Tex Barker. Laura smiled at him, acting glad to see him. He came forward, removing his hat from his slick black hair. He bowed slightly, with a perfection that Dan had to envy.

'Miss Seton, I'm pleased to see you. It's late. May I walk you home?'

'Didn't you come to see the marshal?'

'Not anymore.'

Dan leaned back in his chair as he watched her take the gambler's arm. She smiled back at him as they left. They were a strange pair, he thought.

Since he was now invited to the Creightons' for dinner, Dan shaved, washed his face, and went out into the twilight. He ached all over and was ready for Virginia's good food.

As he walked up the street and along an alley, he thought of how he had caught Virginia when she fell from the chair. Her lips were sweet as cider, and the softness of her was not going to leave his mind. He hadn't planned that moment with her. And if he was going to smoke out the killers, he had better keep his head clear.

He entered the Creightons' house worrying that she had misread his intentions. But when he paused to stare at Josh Hartley, Dan realized the pain in his middle was a competitive rush.

Josh shook his hand, and they stood in front of the newly lit fire in the big hearth. The young man was still pink-faced. No one else was in the room.

'Marshal, I felt like a fool down by the river. They came ridin' up, and I didn't suspect they'd been drinking. Then that Olson grabbed me and put a gun to my head.'

'Could have happened to anyone.'

'I wasn't armed, Marshal. I never believed in guns. I remember there was a lot of killing when I was ten or so. My mother was pretty upset over it and sent me off to my aunt's in

Philadelphia. I went to school, and now I'm studying law. But here I am, right back where men are killing each other.'

'Is your mother out at the ranch?'

'She died a few months after my father.'

'Sorry to hear that. I was hoping they could tell me what happened twelve years ago when the Cassidys were killed.'

'Like I said, I was only ten. But you're welcome to come on out to the ranch. I'm sure my brothers would help you find out anything you want to know. Jedediah's your age, and Judson's nearly thirty. They'll remember something, I'm sure.'

'Are you stayin' out there?'

'I'm at the hotel right now.'

Virginia entered the room. She was wearing a frilly apron over her blue dress. Her golden hair was twirled back in waves, but a loose lock dangled near her left eye. There was flour on her nose.

She offered them coffee as Creighton came down the stairs. The three men stood around the hearth and talked until they were called to dinner. At the table they sat down to delicious roast beef and potatoes with gravy.

Virginia turned to Dan, who sat at her right. 'Dan, don't you think Josh will make a fine lawyer?'

'He looks the part,' Dan said.

Josh puffed up a little. 'There's an outfit just set up last fall called the American Bar Association. I sure aim to be a member.'

The conversation turned to ready-print from Denver. Virginia blushed when her uncle protested the corset ads that bragged about using coralline instead of whalebone. She pushed for the advertisements for Arm & Hammer Baking Soda, which, he pointed out, ran jointly with a cure for ulcerated sores and other unmentionables.

Embarrassed, she turned to Josh and

asked about Philadelphia, in particular about the museums. Josh entertained them with stories about politics and how he had just read Mark Twain's *Roughing It*. He had been to concerts and the theater. Dan envied the way Josh kept Virginia fascinated with his tales, but he liked the young man.

'Miss Seton went to school in Philadelphia,' Virginia said. 'Did you know her?'

'No, but no Seton wants anything to do with a Hartley,' Josh said. 'Anyhow, before I go back, I want to go up north to Yellowstone Park. There's fire spitting out of the ground, and water and steam shooting into the sky.'

Creighton grunted. 'Don't believe all that malarkey. Besides, you could leave your scalp behind. It ain't that far from where Custer got it just three years ago.'

'Well, he does need a haircut,' Virginia said.

There was a lot of laughter among friends that evening. It made Dan feel good, warm. His biggest pleasure was watching Virginia. She had a smile that would shame a sunset.

After supper, they sat around the blazing hearth. Dan turned to the young man.

'Josh, will you ride out with me to see your brothers?'

'Sure, but let me warn you, they're ornery and spoiling for a fight all the time. But I guess it took men like my father and brothers to open up this land. Of course, if you listen to the Setons, they did it all by themselves.'

It was agreed that come morning, Josh would ride with Dan to meet with his brothers. Virginia insisted on coming along. Dan had to admit she was nice company. It would also make his visit less official and less obvious.

But as he headed back for the jail, Dan had misgivings.

He wanted to shout to the rooftops that his name was Cassidy. That would flush them out. But then he would be shot in the back in some dark alley. And the Cassidy line would end.

No, he had to sneak up on them, one by one.

4

The next morning, the trio rode out to the Hartley ranch. Josh was astride a rented bay gelding, and next to him, Virginia rode her bay mare. Her pretty flaxen hair blew in the slight breeze.

Dan's black stallion was aware of the mare, and was acting a bit silly. It was all Dan could do to keep his prancing horse away from the mare.

As the others rode on ahead, following the south side of the river and heading west along the trail, Dan looked at the wooden bridge. The river was some thirty feet wide here, the white water leaping and spraying. As a child, he had loved that wild river.

Virginia reined up and rode back. 'You're lagging behind, Marshal.'

'Just enjoying the country.'

The rolling grassland was spotted with blue and yellow wildflowers. A lazy

68

hawk circled overhead in the clear sky, and the sun warmed them. They passed groves of aspen and cottonwood, interspersed with spots of brush and big rocks. To the north, south, and west, high mountains crested with snow circled most of the valley. Dan remembered coming this way to see the falls.

At midday, they sighted a herd of cattle, and Josh reined up. 'We're getting pretty close to the ranch. But listen, Marshal, like I said, my brothers are a little rough. Don't be taking them too seriously.'

When they reached the ranch house on a knoll, Josh nervously led the way to the corrals. Two older men were working with a green bronc in the larger corral.

One of them came over to greet Josh. 'Your brothers just went up to the house.'

Dan looked the men over. They didn't look like gunmen. Instead, they looked like weary trail hands who had found a comfortable home.

The ranch house was simple inside with a stone fireplace and leather furniture. Hides hung on the walls and covered some of the floor. It was obvious that only men lived here. Josh led the way and offered them chairs.

They could smell coffee, along with sweat and leather, and Josh went into the other room. Virginia sat near Dan and surveyed the place.

'I don't like it here,' she said. 'It's so manly.'

Josh returned with one of his brothers, a stocky man of medium height, and introduced him as Judson. His face was lean, and he had eyes that were darker and meaner than Josh's. He was wearing dirty Levi's and a torn shirt. When he saw Virginia, he acted ill at ease and tipped an imaginary hat. Then he concentrated on Dan, who sensed there were secrets behind those sinister eyes.

'What do you want out here, Marshal?' Judson asked in a none-too-friendly tone.

'Now, Judson, he's just here for a visit,' Josh said.

'Josh, just go sit down. You college boys don't know nothin'.'

Josh's chin went up. 'I ain't a kid no more, Judson.'

It was then that another man entered the room with an iron-gray dog that quietly lay down near the hearth. Josh introduced him as Jedediah. He was younger than Judson, with the same strong features but gentler eyes. He volunteered to bring coffee. As they sat and drank the strong liquid, Jedediah leaned back in his big chair.

Dan gazed at him a long moment. He seemed to remember a boy about his age, down by the river, fishing or swimming.

'So what can we do for you, Marshal?'

'About six months ago, a man named Shanks was murdered.'

'Sure, we heard about that,' Jed replied. 'Probably some miner lookin' for a grubstake. Never knew Shanks to

71

hurt a fly, much less pick a fight.'

'I also wanted some information on the Cassidy murders.'

Jed appeared surprised. 'That was a long time ago. Well, we don't know nothin'. Go talk to the Setons. They ended up with the place. Now Josh, stop gawkin' at this lady, will you?'

Josh was embarrassed even as Virginia smiled. Teasing Josh seemed to be their favorite pastime, although it was obvious they were proud of him.

But Judson was a grouch. 'The Setons think they own the whole valley. And Karl Seton plays around with what he charges at that bank of his. If we need any more money, we're goin' to Denver.'

'Did you know Tom Cassidy?' Dan persisted.

'Saw him in town,' Judson said. 'That's all. Him and his missus and them skinny kids. But he was stirrin' things up, all right, tryin' to organize the small ranchers.'

'You didn't join in?'

Judson grunted. 'Me and Jed, we was too young. But our pa wanted nothin' to do with it.'

Dan stood up slowly. 'Josh, you ridin' back with us?'

'No, I'm moving in here for a few months, afore I go back to school.'

Judson turned to Virginia. 'Your uncle still writin' them editorials?'

'He tries,' she said.

'Someone's gonna take a potshot at him.'

Virginia frowned, and walked quickly outside with Dan. Josh followed them into the sunlight, and hurriedly went to assist her into the saddle, flirting as he helped her swing astride.

Dan and Virginia rode off together, heading back to town. Dan found that he was glad that Josh had stayed behind, but he was nervous riding next to her. She was excited about every bird, animal, and flower that she saw. He liked watching her. She made him feel fifteen years old again.

When they reached the river trail, it

was late afternoon. They saw ten riders on the other side of the wide, shallow water.

'It's the Setons,' she said. 'That's Kirk and some of his men, and that awful Char Olson. Giles Seton's that older man in front.'

Dan reined up, face burning.

Giles Seton was directly across the river, riding free and sitting tall in the saddle, looking as if he owned the whole state of Colorado. The man had white hair and a paunch, and a hard face with a jutting jaw. His heavy coat was open, showing his gun belt.

Without noticing them, the riders continued on down the river toward town. Sweat ran down Dan's face. His hand was so tight on the reins, he felt pain, for he was convinced the Setons had killed his family.

'Dan, are you all right?' Virginia asked anxiously.

'I'd better have a talk with your uncle.'

As they rode back, all Dan could

think of was his secret, which he knew must not die with him. When they reached the town, there was no sign of the Setons. They left the horses at the livery and walked along a back street.

'Are we hiding?' she asked.

He shook his head. When he saw Giles, he had suddenly realized how vulnerable he was. He had only Hammer on his side. He could be shot in the back. And he didn't want Virginia to be a target while walking with him.

At the newspaper office, they found Sid Creighton running some handbills for Tex Barker advertising that he had the best liquor in town. Wearily, the editor stopped and greeted them.

'Well, Dan, did you meet Josh's brothers? Aren't they a pair of tough ones?'

Dan nodded. 'Seems like no one around here knows anything. Listen. We have to talk, and you two are the only ones I can trust.'

'Let's go to the house then.'

Creighton locked up the office, and

they headed up the slope. Virginia glanced at Dan curiously as he walked at her side. At the house, they sat down with reheated coffee around the kitchen table. Dan slowly pulled the letter from his pocket and handed it to them.

As they read it, Creighton looked up. 'What does this mean?'

'I'm Dan Cassidy.'

Creighton's jaw dropped in astonishment and Virginia looked stunned.

Dan continued as tears welled up in his eyes. 'I was in the cellar with my little sister when it happened. I was the only one to get out alive. Shanks hid me and convinced me to change my name, then he sent me off to Texas. I didn't think I'd ever learn who did it — until I got this letter. Like it says, Shanks heard some drunk making a confession. I figure right after he sent this letter, Shanks was killed for what he knew.'

'So what are you figuring?' Creighton asked.

'Without Shanks, that letter ain't much use. I need live witnesses, and someone might talk if I hang around long enough. And I'm convinced the Setons were behind the killings.'

The editor shrugged. 'You know, Dan, you're taking on too much here.'

'I want you to keep this letter in case something happens to me. Just get it back to Denver to Marshal Wilcox, who's the law there. He'll send someone else.'

'All right. I'll keep it for you.'

They insisted that Dan stay for supper. Virginia heated up stew and made biscuits. She looked worried and anxious. When he left later that night, she followed him outside and stood near him in the moonlight.

'Oh, Dan, it must have been awful for you. A fifteen-year-old boy losing everything like that.'

Agony gripped him. He wanted to tell her his misery, but his grief still choked him after all these years.

He moved to the steps, then paused. He had the urge to reach for her, but he turned away. Just then, her hand caught his. He paused, surprised, as she fell into his arms, her face on his chest. He held her against his pounding heart and touched her silken hair with a clumsy hand.

Her hands dug into his back as he felt her tremble. When she finally lifted her head, he saw tears on her cheeks.

'Dan, I wish I could erase it all for you.'

He couldn't help himself, seeing the compassion in her wet eyes. His own tears were brimming as he bent his head and pressed his lips gently to hers. She tenderly kissed him back, sensing his pain and sharing it.

Abruptly, he released her and quickly headed down the steps, biting his lip and not looking back.

Back in the house, Virginia dried her eyes with her lace handkerchief. Then she found her uncle in the kitchen. He was busy with a pencil, writing on a large sheet of old newsprint.

'What are you writing?'

'Honey, I'm a newspaper man. I got

to finish the work I started yesterday.'

She bent over and kissed his cheek. 'Remember, you're all I have, so please get some rest.'

He looked up with a grunt, but his eyes were twinkling. She wondered if he knew how much she loved him, but she went up to her room, too weary to sit with him.

In her bed, eyes closed, she again felt Dan's arms around her, his kiss like fire on her lips. She wondered if he could ride away and never look back.

★ ★ ★

In the morning, Creighton wasn't in the house when Virginia came downstairs, and she assumed he was already at work. Before noon, she went to make his bed and was startled to find it had not been slept in. But then he often worked all night. She filled a jar with hot coffee and put it in a small box with some biscuits.

Outside, she discovered it was cooler

than expected. The sky was streaked with clouds. A breeze ruffled her dress and lifted her hair as she went downhill toward the office.

An elderly woman in a sunbonnet and cape was standing on the corner of the main street, holding a newspaper. She looked up and lowered the pages.

'Oh, Miss Creighton. Did you see your uncle's editorial this morning?'

'You mean the paper's out?'

'All over town. He had a boy passing them out long before sunrise. You know, your uncle is going to make someone mad one of these days.'

Virginia nodded and turned away, heading toward the newspaper office. She found the back door locked. Suddenly nervous, she fought in her purse for her key. The box fell from her hand, coffee spilling, but she paid it no mind.

Jerking the door open, she found lamps still burning. The hand-operated press hadn't been cleaned. Type and newsprint were scattered all over. A fire had been started in a wastebasket, but had burned out without spreading. The front door was ajar.

And on the floor lay her uncle, staring lifeless at the ceiling. In one hand, he still clutched a copy of his newspaper, his gnarled fingers white and stiff.

With a gasp, she knelt beside him, touching his cold face. Tears flushed her eyes and trickled down her burning cheeks. He had been her only family, her whole life, a man she had followed everywhere.

Frantic, she picked up one of the papers and ran out the front door onto the street, so dazed she could barely see. Not many people were about, but discarded papers were blowing across the dirt, curling around hitching rails or being trod on by riders and wagons. The sky had darkened, and it was drizzling.

She ran across the street and up the boardwalk, nearly colliding with an old man and his wife. She nearly fell twice but made it to the jail and thrust the door open to find Hammer having his coffee at the desk.

'My uncle's been murdered in his office.'

'Ma'am, I'm sorry, but the marshal's out of town.'

'Where did he go?'

'He rode out before dawn with Miss Seton and her brother. Please, sit down. I'll go look after your uncle.'

Sick and shaken, tears streaming down her face, she sat on the marshal's chair as Hammer left the office, closing the door behind him.

She wiped away her tears, choking on them. Then she lifted the newspaper to read what her uncle had written, terrified to know how far he had gone this time.

She read it slowly. It began with the story of the attempt on Dan's life, followed by the usual inflammatory arguments for law and order. But then he had added:

There have been unsolved murders in this valley for over a decade. This editor calls on every citizen in town to take any information on the perpetrators to the marshal. It's time we took back our town and our valley. Tell the marshal. Tell him now.

5

It had taken Dan, Karl, and Laura all morning to cross the vast acres of the Seton ranch. Hunched up in the saddle, his slicker protecting him from the rain and chill, Dan was beginning to realize how much land the Setons had managed to seize. Herds of their cattle roamed the hills as far as the eye could see.

He didn't know how he would react when he came face-to-face with Giles Seton. He only knew he had to withhold his anger and thirst for vengeance until more evidence fell in his hands.

'Isn't it lovely?' Laura asked, waving her gloved hand at the distant hills. She rode sidesaddle, her red hair topped with a white hat and feathers.

'Just a lot of grass,' Karl said.

'Oh, Karl, you've become too much

of a city slicker.'

When they sighted the ranch buildings, Dan was impressed with the size of the corrals and outbuildings. The house was two stories high, set on a knoll overlooking its domain.

They dismounted, leaving their horses at the corral, and walked into the house. Dan paused to stare at a painting over the giant hearth. It was a picture of Giles Seton on a gray horse. Looking like a general, he was stern and foreboding.

They were greeted by Mrs. Seton, a small gray-haired woman who promptly offered them cookies and coffee. They sat on plush chairs as she fussed over them.

'The marshal came to meet Father,' Laura said.

'Oh, dear, your father's out hunting with Kirk. Maybe they'll be back in a few hours. Can you wait?'

Dan shrugged, shaking his head.

Laura and her mother went into the kitchen. Dan felt strange, sitting in the house of the man who may have ordered his family's murders. He grew red with frustration, and tried to control himself as Karl spoke.

'So, do you want to wait for my father?'

'Not for long.'

'You know, Marshal, you seem awfully curious about the Setons. My father's gettin' on in years. I hope you won't upset him.'

Abruptly, there was a pounding on the front door. Karl got to his feet and went to answer it. A cowhand stood on the porch, out of breath, with a newspaper in his hand. Behind him, his horse was drenched with sweat.

'Mr. Seton, is your pa here? I brung him this paper. You'd better see he reads it.'

Karl took the newspaper and turned slowly as he closed the door, reading it as he walked back to his chair. He slumped down, shaking his head.

'Creighton's just trying to stir things up. I don't know why we even need a newspaper in town.'

He handed it to Dan, who also stared at the words. Creighton may have gone too far this time. The man had a talent for being inflammatory. The editor didn't name anyone, but it was obvious he was talking about the big ranchers, and Seton was the biggest. And he was asking everyone who knew anything to step forward. The guilty would have to silence him.

'I've got to get back,' Dan said, rising.

Karl and Laura waited until the door closed behind Dan. Through the window, Karl watched until the marshal was on his stallion and heading back toward town.

Then Karl turned to his sister, eyes gleaming.

'I thought you were going to work on him, Laura. I want you to find out all he knows about Rawhide and this valley.'

'You have to give me time. Unless you want me to stop being a lady,' she answered sharply.

'I don't care how you do it.'

'Karl, I never heard such talk.'

'Don't give me your fancy schoolin'. You're a Seton, so you'd better do just what I say if you don't want to see your pa and brothers hang.'

'Hang for what?'

'Never you mind. Just go after Casey, that's all.'

★ ★ ★

Meanwhile, Dan rode quickly toward town, holding his hat against the wind and rain. The editor had written other controversial editorials, but Dan's instincts told him this would cause real trouble.

Dan called on the stallion's great strength and endurance, covering the trail in half the time. By twilight, he was already crossing the wooden bridge into Rawhide. The street was empty.

He headed straight for the newspaper office. Lamps were burning inside, but the shades were drawn. Creighton was all right, that wonderful fool, but Dan might have to lock him up for his own safety.

He dismounted and loosened the cinch, leaving his weary stallion at the railing. Anxiously, he knocked on the door.

'Who is it?' Virginia called.

'Dan. Let me in.'

He heard the bar being dropped, and the door opened. She was framed against the lamplight. There was ink all over her oversize apron as well as her nose and cheeks. She stepped aside, letting him enter, then barred the door.

The place was a mess. Type lay all over the floor, and paper was bunched up as if swept aside. It was obvious she had been setting type. He turned to look at her reddened eyes.

'Where's your uncle?'

'They killed him, Dan!'

With a sob, she fell into his arms. He held her, feeling her tremors right through him. He knew her pain, her misery, her helplessness. He pressed his hand to her golden hair and kept her in his arms until she finally broke free.

She turned to the type tray. Her tears were flowing.

'This is my editorial, Dan.'

'Are you out of your mind? You can't run the newspaper.'

'Why not?'

'Because you'll get hurt. Someone will take a shot at you for sure. How can you defend yourself?'

She wiped her tears with the back of her hand. 'I can use a six-shooter. There's one in the drawer somewhere.'

'Virginia, you can't take any chances.'

'I just want to push for law and order.' She continued to place the type, a determined set to her jaw.

'Well, your uncle did everything but accuse the Setons outright. You can't go on doing that.'

Helpless, Dan stood a long while, watching her work. He had never known a woman so brave — and so stubborn. After a moment, he came forward and took her arm, gently but firmly.

'Whatever you're printin' can wait a few days. I'll walk you home.'

She leaned back, shaken and weary. 'You're right. I just had to take some action.'

'Is anyone staying with you?'

'Yes — Molly Denson, the sheriff's widow.'

'When's the funeral?'

'We already had it, Dan.'

There was a sudden knock on the door. Virginia turned pale, obviously nervous and afraid. Dan moved to the side of the door and opened it cautiously until he saw Hammer standing out front. He let the big man inside and closed the door again.

'Marshal, I seen your horse outside. I been walkin' the town, like you said. And I thought you'd like to know a bunch of Seton's hard cases rode in. Three of 'em. They're at the Four Star Café up the street.'

'Know any of them?'

'No, but they look pretty mean. I sure wouldn't want to cross any one of them. They're carrying a lot of iron.'

'All right. You take Miss Creighton home. I'll just have a look.'

'No, Dan,' Virginia said, touching his arm.

Dan turned toward the door, but paused, looking back at her. 'It's all right. Hammer, you take her home.'

Seeing the haunted look on her face, Dan felt her pain as if it were his own. But he had to go out into the darkness.

When he reached the Four Star Café, he saw three horses tied to the railing. Each saddle carried a Winchester repeater and heavy saddlebags, probably loaded with ammunition.

Dan peered through the greasy windows. He could see a group of men at a table by the far wall. Two other men who appeared to be merchants were seated in the center, having their supper.

Casually, Dan entered and walked to a table. He sat down with his back to the wall, opposite the strangers' table. He nodded to the merchants, then ordered steak and beans with coffee. He didn't look toward the hard cases, but he knew they were watching him. His badge gleamed in the lamplight as wind shook the windows and rattled the door.

The waitress was a redhead with a pretty face and dimples. As she refilled his coffee cup and brought him his food, she smiled down at him.

'My late husband was a lawman. Right here in Rawhide.'

Startled, Dan realized she was the sheriff's widow, Molly Denson, who was staying with Virginia to console her. Dan liked her right away.

'Sorry to hear that, ma'am.'

'Call me Molly. But it's all right, Marshal. My husband was a good man, but I didn't know he'd been killed. I came out on the stage a few weeks ago and didn't have enough money to go home. The doctor had written me, but I never got the letters. He met me at the stage and took me to his home. I got this job three days ago.'

'Well, I'm sorry about your husband.'

She shook her head. 'It wasn't right, Marshal. And a month before my husband was killed, another man was shot down in the same alley. A Mr. Shanks.'

'The alley next to the gambling hall?'

She nodded. 'Enjoy your meal, Marshal. And please be careful.'

Dan finished eating, never looking directly at the Seton gunmen. As he enjoyed a refill of hot coffee, he could see from the corner of his eye that one of them was coming over.

When the man was directly across the table, Dan slowly leaned back and shoved his hat up to get a better look. He was tall and lean, with a slick moustache and a scar on his left cheek. He wore a fancy vest and a cut-down holster, and looked to be in his mid-thirties. Suddenly he recognized the man. It was Carmody, a gunman who had covered his back in a fight in

Austin so long ago. He had saved Dan's life.

'I thought it was you, Casey. Mind if I sit?'

Dan shook his head, watching carefully as Carmody sat down. Dan glanced over at the other two men.

'I see you still have that ugly Mace with you,' he said.

Carmody smiled. 'Yes, he's a mean one. And maybe you remember Buck. Havin' them around makes me feel like I'm better than them, and that's a rare feelin' these days. Well now, a federal badge, I see. You're a long way from Texas.'

'So are you.'

'Man pays us well.'

'Seton?'

Carmody leaned back. 'Who else?'

Dan studied Carmody, who had brought his coffee with him. They sipped the hot liquid, taking measure of each other. Carmody was obviously trying to learn just how far he could go. But the gunman didn't seem to be looking for a fight just now.

'Why does Seton need you, anyway?' Dan asked.

'He's a worried man. He likes to surround himself with his own little army.'

'Worried about what?'

'A man who has everything is likely to be fearful of someone stealin' it from him.'

'It doesn't sound like your kind of job.'

'Pay is more than I've seen in a year. So if I just have to sit around and wait, that's fine with me.'

'Sort of retirement?'

'Just about. I just eat and sleep and walk around town wearin' these side arms and lookin' tough. Scares people, I reckon, and that's what Seton wants. What about you, Dan? Why are you in this forsaken place?'

'It's just part of my territory. And there were some murders here. Six months ago, a fellow named Shanks was killed. And Sheriff Denson was shot down a month later. And twelve years ago, the Cassidy family. Know anything about that?'

'We've only been here a couple months.'

'What about Creighton?'

Carmody shrugged. 'Don't know about that. But listen, Dan, if I had my druthers, I'd be sittin' on some mountaintop with my traps on line and my rifle across my knee, staring out where no other man walked for miles. And maybe I'd marry that Cheyenne woman I was so crazy about up north. But that ain't gonna happen, Dan. I'm makin' too much money. And I got me a reputation, and they won't let it lie. There ain't no way I'm gonna be able to quit.'

Dan watched Carmody's sudden bitterness exposed, and he felt sorry for the man. Carmody was as stuck with his lot as Dan was with his own.

The gunman downed his coffee and looked serious. 'Watch your back, Dan.'

Carmody stood up and turned to join

his men. Mace was the ugly one, with the crooked mouth, a cigarette dangling from his fat lips, his left eye half closed. Buck had a missing front tooth and near white eyes.

After they left, Hammer came inside. He was carrying a rifle, and looked worried. He sat down opposite Dan, barely fitting in the chair, and ordered a meal.

'Marshal, that was a mean-lookin' bunch.'

'The leader's Carmody. Hired gun, but no back shooter.'

'If you was to face him head on, could you beat him?'

Dan shrugged. 'I wouldn't want to bet on it.'

'Did you get to meet Giles Seton?'

'No, he wasn't there, and when I saw the newspaper, I rushed back. But I was too late.'

Hammer shook his head. 'Creighton sure knew how to put the words together. I guess he just made 'em mad this time.'

Uneasy, Dan glanced down at the star on his vest. He had thought it would bring him power to right the wrongs. Yet he was helpless without evidence.

When Hammer was served, Dan watched him devour two steaks. He liked this gentle giant. When he finished, they went back out into the dark rain. The street was empty except for a wagon with no team. A dog snarled at them from the alley. They made their way carefully through the mud and over to the jail. Out of the cold and wet, they turned up the lamps and put a fire in the stove. Hammer put on a fresh pot of coffee.

Later that night, Dan looked out the window and noticed a lamp burning in the newspaper office. He crossed the wet, muddy street and pounded at the door. After a moment Virginia let him in. She wore the same ink-covered apron over her green dress.

She watched him bar the door, then turned to finish her typesetting.

'I thought I sent you home,' Dan said.

Virginia ignored the accusation in his words. 'Did you find out who killed my uncle?'

'No.'

'And you won't be able to find out who killed your family, Dan. Even if it were Giles Seton, he owns half this town. No one will testify against him. The only thing you'll find is a bullet in your back. You should leave Rawhide right away.'

'What about you?'

'I'm staying to finish what my uncle started.'

'I'm riding out to the Setons. You keep your doors locked. And don't be printing anything that'll get you hurt.'

She turned very slowly, her eyes brimming, but her chin high. 'You can't stop me. Just you worry about yourself, Dan Casey.'

They stood glaring at each other, but inwardly he wanted to reach for her, to hold her and ease her pain. Instead, he just stood there, baffled by her determination.

Finally, he turned and unbarred the door, going back outside. He heard her put the bar in place. Then he drew himself up and proceeded down the street. It was mighty cold, and a chill went right through him.

He went to the livery, retrieved his stallion, saddled, and mounted. He rode out toward the bridge.

Dawn was almost breaking before he sighted the great herds of Seton cattle, huddled under trees and in hollows. When he came over the next rise, he saw the ranch house and corrals.

Despite the cold, he felt sweat on his back.

At the Seton ranch house, Dan reined up next to another horse at the railing. He twisted in the saddle, and saw that the corrals were filled with saddle horses.

He walked up on the porch and pounded once on the big oak door. Finally, he heard a latch moving. The door swung open.

Laura Seton stared at him, then smiled. She was pretty in her white shawl, her red hair drawn back.

'Why, Marshal, come in out of the rain. We have a fire going. I'll get you some coffee.'

'Where's your father?' he asked abruptly, removing his hat as he stepped inside. He allowed her to take his slicker and hang it on a rack. A roaring fire was in the hearth. She led him toward the warmth.

'Father and my brothers are out at the bunkhouse.'

He had barely turned his back to the flames when she moved up against him, sliding her hands up to his face. Caught off guard, he felt a strange wave of fear run through him. She caught him by the neck and pulled his face down to hers.

Before he could catch his breath, she was kissing him soundly. But he couldn't respond. Feeling uneasy, he stood with his arms at his sides.

She drew back slowly, her hands sliding down his chest.

'Is that the best you can do?' she asked.

'Did you read that newspaper article?'

Annoyed, she backed away. 'Well, yes, but you can't believe all that innuendo. And that's all it is, Dan. Speculation.' With a toss of her red hair, she went for the coffee, bringing two steaming cups. They sat down in front of the fire.

'Marshal, it doesn't do much for my confidence for you to be here only on business,' Laura said.

'Creighton was murdered.'

She looked surprised. 'I'm sorry to hear that. But maybe if you'd tell me why you're in town, I could help.'

Dan leaned back to study her, wondering if she was being mighty smart.

'I came here to investigate Shanks's murder, and now the sheriff's. And the Cassidys', twelve years ago.'

'Have you learned anything?'

Abruptly, the door opened. Karl came in out of the rain, pulling his wet hat from his head. He grunted at Dan as he removed his slicker and came over to the fire to warm himself. Laura left to get him some coffee.

'So you're back, Marshal. Is it because of that crazy newspaper article?'

'Sid Creighton was murdered.'

Karl shrugged and sat down. 'Listen, Marshal, we don't know anything about that.'

'Where's your father?'

Then the door opened. Giles Seton came inside, shaking off the rain. His white hair and hard face were dripping wet. Deep lines crossed the sides of his mouth and his brow. Cold gray eyes squinted as he took off his slicker and started toward the fire. Then he paused, taking a good look at Dan.

Dan's gut wrenched with pent-up fury. Agony gripped his every muscle. Instinctively, Dan believed this man was responsible for his family's murders, yet he couldn't prove it. His heart was beating so fast, he thought it would break free of his chest.

'Marshal,' Laura asked, 'are you ill?'

Dan drew a deep breath as Giles approached them. He had to control his urge to charge the man, to beat him to the floor, to pound him until he admitted the truth.

Karl turned to Dan. 'My sister's right, Marshal. You look ill.'

Dan swallowed hard, his chest burning. 'No, I'm all right.'

'I'll bet you haven't eaten,' Laura said. 'My mother's asleep, but I'll fix you something.'

Dan shook his head. 'No, this is business. Mr. Seton, Creighton was murdered.'

Giles Seton stood by the fire, tall and arrogant.

'Why come to me?'

'I thought you might know who did it.'

'My business is cattle.'

Dan set his cup on the table and stood up, facing him squarely. He was taller than the fierce rancher.

'I heard you didn't like what Creighton was printing.'

'Never did. I tried to buy him out. I don't like anyone stirrin' things up in my valley. In fact, I'd like it fine if everyone was gone but us Setons. I got here first, Marshal. I run off the Indians. I fought the rustlers and nesters. And still they come crowdin' me like locusts.'

'If your business is cattle, why did you hire Carmody?'

'We're hirin' on for the roundup. You got a problem with that?'

'Maybe.'

'If that's all you come for, you can be on your way.'

'You can tell me about the Cassidy killings.'

'I don't know nothin' about that.'

'You had plenty to gain by it.'

'So did the Hartleys and every other big rancher in the valley.'

'But you got the Cassidy land.'

'By public auction.'

Dan shrugged, then pulled on his hat. He hesitated a moment, trying to control his need to drag the truth out of these men.

But he drew himself up and left. He mounted his stallion in the rain and rode toward the big bunkhouse. Kirk Seton was coming out, his hat pulled down on his brow. His ruddy face was set in a frown, his red mustache twitching as he drew his slicker about him.

'Marshal, what are you doing here?'

'Creighton was murdered.'

'Sorry to hear that.'

'How many men you have on this spread?'

'Roundup's comin', Marshal. We got five old-timers and twenty new ones to help get 'em out of the brush and mark and brand 'em.'

'You know Carmody?'

'Sure. He works for us.'

'Ever see him turn a cow?'

'We need all kinds of men here, Marshal.'

Sweat running down his neck, Dan rode on, sitting tall in the saddle yet disgusted that he had learned nothing.

Kirk strode over to the ranch house, joining Karl, who had come out onto the porch. Rain dripped from their hat brims as they faced each other. Both men were their father's sons. His stubborn boldness, wild determination, and family pride ran hot in their veins. They wanted this valley as much as Giles, and nothing was going to stop them. Not even the law.

'Blast it, Karl, you're too nice to that lawman.'

'Always be nice to a man before he dies.'

'What's that mean?'

Karl grunted. 'Casey's too blamed nosy. He's going to be a problem if he sticks around.'

'I could take him,' Kirk said. 'I'm the fastest gun in this valley. Faster than you, Karl. And I bet I could take

Carmody himself.'

'Well, we ain't takin' no chances. And we don't want the law comin' after any Setons.'

'So what are you going to do?'

'Our boys will take the shortcut. Casey's a dead man.'

6

On his way back from the Seton Ranch, Dan was despondent. The trauma of having met the man he believed was responsible for his family's murders was too much for him. The meeting had left him a shambles, so much so that even two hours later he didn't see the oncoming rider until he was within fifty yards.

It was Tex Barker, the gambler, still a dandy even in a slicker. They reined up to face each other.

'Well, Marshal, you're a busy man.'

'You headed out to the Setons?'

'Thought I'd pay my respects to Miss Seton. Maybe I'll even be invited to stay. Giles seems to like me all right. I make a lot of money, and he respects that.'

Dan gazed at him a long while. 'I got me a feeling you came to Rawhide for reasons other than making money.'

'Maybe I'll fill you in some day.'

'You don't come across as a gambler.'

'Don't bet on it.'

With that, Barker smiled, tipped his hat, and rode on. Dan turned in the saddle to watch him cross over the hillside. Then he slowly urged on his stallion. He still had another two hours before he reached the bridge.

He could vaguely see Seton cattle off in the distance, but the rain clouded the valley and cut his vision. He rode through a grove of aspen and headed around some of the rocks that lined the trail.

Suddenly, a bullet whistled by his ear. He spun his stallion around and dove for cover behind the rocks. Whoever was shooting, they were in the boulders beyond the trail.

Seizing his rifle from the scabbard, Dan dismounted, drawing his Colt and huddling down in the rocks.

Just as he ducked behind the stone, a bullet came from his left, past his arm.

Rifles were aimed at him from two directions. Then another shot rang out from the aspens, and another bullet cut past his head from behind. He ducked lower into the rocks. He was surrounded by four men. His stallion nervously tossed its head.

Dan swallowed hard. So Giles Seton had set his men after him. There couldn't be any other answer, not way out here on the trail. Dan wondered if he was going to die without ever avenging his family.

The four rifles spat at him. He realized they could have killed him easily at first, but now they were playing with him like a cat with its prey. Down between the rocks, Dan tried to avoid being a target. Yet to defend himself, he would have to rise. Only the man in the aspens appeared vulnerable.

Dan sighted him, rearing up a little, and fired. Then he dropped down quickly, but not before he saw the man jerk backward and crash to the ground.

That left three: one in the rocks in

front of him, one somewhere in the brush to his left, and another behind him. He decided to stay put and let them come after him.

Abruptly, the man in the rocks moved for a better shot. Before Dan could fire, a lone rifle cracked from beyond the aspens.

The gunman, hit in the chest, rose up and fell face-down into the grass, arms outstretched.

The man in the brush started firing rapidly in the direction of the shot, but he had to rise to do it. The man beyond the trees fired again, the bullet hitting the ambusher square between the eyes. He disappeared in the brambles.

Dan turned to look behind him, and discovered that the fourth gunman was charging him, rifle at the ready.

Dan fired, hitting him in the chest. The man staggered backward with a cry and dropped to his knees. He tried to raise his rifle, then collapsed.

Hesitating a moment, Dan peered toward the aspens. Rain made it difficult to see who had come to his aid. Then he saw the rider come forward. It was Tex Barker.

Dan stood up and mounted his stallion, riding out to meet Tex. The gambler was grinning, resting his elbow on the saddle horn. 'Tell me, Marshal, is this an ordinary day for you?'

Dan shrugged, pulling his hat down tight. 'I have to thank you for helping me out.'

'I was on my way back. I heard the shots up the trail.'

Dan studied him. 'I can't figure you out.'

'I got to thinking about the Seton family squabble and turned around. A prudent man doesn't get caught in that kind of trouble. I'll just ride back with you.'

'You recognize any of these men?'

'Nope, but the Setons been hirin' for roundup.'

Dan rode around the fallen men, looked them over, then dismounted to look for identification. There was none, but each carried a ten-dollar gold coin, which Dan shoved back in their pockets. These men had followed instructions: They had been ordered not to carry identification in case they were caught.

Dan mounted and rode southeast along the trail with Tex. He would let Seton bury his own — if they were indeed his.

Dan peered sideways at the gambler. 'I surely do like the way you're taking care of me.'

'You're still wet behind the ears, Marshal. Someone's got to look after you.'

'You're forgettin' Hammer.'

'He's big all right. But he's not too smart.'

When they reached the bridge, it was early afternoon. Tex went on to his place, and Dan headed down to the jail, where he found Hammer making fresh coffee. The room felt warm and snug. Dan hung his slicker on the rack and shook the rain from his hat.

'Everything quiet?'

'Not anymore. There's trouble at the gambling hall. That Char Olson and a couple of gunmen are makin' a lot of noise.'

'I'm too tired and hungry to think on it. Have you seen Miss Creighton?'

'Have I? Look at this.'

Dan stiffened as his deputy held up a newspaper. Grimly, he reached over and took it from the man's hands. He sat down and stared at the words, which were not quite as inflammatory as Creighton's. Just the same, she was demanding law and order and information about her uncle's murder.

He was reaching for his slicker just as the door opened and Virginia came inside. She carried a basket, which she set on the table. She was wet and pretty, but Dan was so worried about her that he hardly smelled the fresh cookies that Hammer was already munching.

Dan shook the newspaper at her. 'You know they killed your uncle because he wrote like this. Now you're doing it. I'm locking you up for your own safety.'

Her chin went up. 'No, you are not.'

'You'll get everybody in the valley mad at you.'

'I'm not giving up the paper. And I'm certainly not sitting in any cell.'

'We'll see about that.'

Dan caught her wrist and pulled her through the door to the cells as she fought him.

'Dan Casey, you let go of me!'

She kicked at him furiously as he dragged her, fighting all the way, to the end cell.

She caught the cell door and clung to it. He tried to pull her free, but she kicked at him.

He grabbed her by the waist and jerked her free, but she fell against him. He staggered backward with the impact, lost his footing, and landed with a crash.

Virginia collapsed on top of him, her fist pounding at his chest. Lying across him, she suddenly caught her breath, gazing down at his embarrassed face.

Then she burst into laughter. She rolled away from him but remained prone, still laughing. Dan turned on his side, rising on his elbow, still glaring at the lovely young woman with the flushed face.

Then he reached out and pulled her back against his chest. He bent his head and kissed her heartily, his lips hot on hers. Her breath was warm and sweet on his face as he drew back. Then they both laughed.

And they looked up at the dismayed Hammer. Dan sat up, took her hand, then rose to his feet and pulled her up with him. He stood holding her cold fingers as he reset his hat.

'Dan,' she said softly, 'I just can't be in a cell.'

'So what am I going to do with you?'

'I'll be all right. Molly's staying with me.'

'And tomorrow, what else are you going to print?'

'What Mr. Barker told me.'

'And what was that?'

She hesitated, gazing at him awkwardly. 'That Tom Cassidy was his brother. That he's your uncle.'

'What?' Dan's heart stopped.

Hammer looked stunned. 'You're a Cassidy, Marshal?'

'He doesn't know who you are, because I thought you should be the one to tell him. But he's setting himself up as a target,' Virginia said.

Dan stared at her. 'We had no other kin.'

'He was the black sheep of the family. He left home when he was barely fourteen, with the law after him. Your father's family had disowned him. After he heard his parents had died, Barker tried for years to find your father. When he did, it was too late.'

Dan tried to swallow everything she said. He released her hand and walked awkwardly back to the office. He sat on the swivel chair, too weak to stand. Tex Barker had acted, walked, and sounded familiar. Now he knew why. Needles ran through Dan's veins as he tried to grasp her words.

'Dan, he wants me to print that his real name is Tex Cassidy,' Virginia said.

Dan shook his head, unable to speak.

'He's been here five years, Dan, and hasn't found out anything. Now he thinks that if they learn he's a Cassidy and here to find the killers, it will flush them out. And he thinks he can survive it because there's a U.S. Marshal in town. Dan, you have to tell him who you are.'

Dan put his hands over his eyes and rested his elbows on the desk. He felt sick. Dismay rushed through his veins. His eyes were wet, stinging. All of his family had not died. Tex Barker — Tex Cassidy — was his uncle. They were both here on the same mission. Dan wasn't alone anymore, and it felt odd, exhilarating, and crushing. A million mixed emotions filled him. But Tex didn't know that Dan Cassidy was alive.

Virginia's hand rested softly on his shoulder. He swallowed and straightened, running his hand across his eyes, then leaned back in the chair. His voice sounded strange.

'No wonder he's been courtin' Laura Seton. He's trying to find out through her.'

Hammer was still surprised. 'I can't believe you're a Cassidy.'

'But don't tell anyone,' Virginia said.

'You hold up that editorial,' Dan told her. 'Maybe Tex and I will let you tell our story at the same time, and then you'll be put somewhere safe. But I have to talk with him first. I still ain't convinced he's tellin' the truth.'

Hammer plunked down in a chair, shaking his head.

'Then,' she said, 'I'd better get back and — '

'I said I was going to lock you up. That editorial you put out today isn't going to make you any friends. They'll want to shut you up even more now.'

'Karl Seton won't let them. He's fond of me.'

'He could have helped murder my family. He and his brother Kirk, and Judson and Jed Hartley, they were all old enough to have been on the raids.'

She frowned. 'Oh, Dan, I hope you're wrong.'

They heard shots up the street. Dan straightened.

Virginia panicked. 'Dan, please don't go. You know they're just waiting for you.'

'You stay in this office and keep the door barred until we come back. Hammer, you come with me.'

Dan swallowed his thoughts of Tex Barker. Right now, he had to think about staying alive. He pulled on his leather coat, tugged his hat down tight, and took up the shotgun. He went outside into the rain, Hammer at his heels with a rifle. He paused long enough to hear her bar the door.

At the gambling hall, he paused by the smeared windows and peered inside. Several men, including Char Olson, were at a center table playing poker. Another group sat at a back table. The room was filled with smoke and the smell of liquor. No one was firing a gun inside. He suspected it had been done in the street or alley to draw him here.

Two gunmen, swarthy and beady-eyed, leaned on the bar, savoring their whiskey as they waited patiently.

As they neared the swinging doors, Dan motioned Hammer to wait outside. Dan looked through the ornate doors into the plush hall. There was no sign of Tex Barker.

Olson was arguing loudly. Then he stood up, turned, and fired his six-gun, putting a bullet in a painting, right between the eyes of a Confederate general.

Olson laughed. It was a loud, blood-curdling laugh like no other, but one Dan knew from somewhere. Then he remembered.

It was the same piercing, brutal

sound Dan had heard the night of the murderous raid. His heart began to beat so fast, he could barely contain himself as he stepped into the gambling hall. Moving slowly with the shotgun, he stepped to his right to keep a wall behind him.

'All right, Olson. Drop your gun.'

Olson turned with a sneer on his fat mouth, cigarette dangling from his lips, his beady eyes gleaming with delight. He holstered his six-gun slowly. Now he stood away from the table, hands at his sides.

The two swarthy gun hands slowly moved to either side of the room. The other men scrambled for cover or ran out the back door. The bartender ducked out of sight.

'Marshal,' Olson said with a slippery smile, 'anyone would think you were afraid of me. You really need that shotgun?'

Dan was stiff, numb all over. The man was challenging him. He could lock him up, only to face him another time. Hammer was outside and could take at least one of the gunmen, most likely the one on the left. Dan might be able to get Char Olson, but could he take the man on the right?

'Well, Marshal?'

Olson spread his feet, grinning. Dan saw Tex come down the back stairs.

Dan's mouth was dry. 'How long have you worked for the Setons?'

'Fifteen years,' Olson said.

'And you were in on the Cassidy murders?'

'Now, Marshal, you're jumpin' to conclusions. What you'd better be thinkin' about right now is whether I'm faster than you. Now that first time, when I shot at you from the alley, I was just funnin'. But I ain't funnin' now, Marshal.'

Maybe it was the certain knowledge that this man was a brutal sadist who had laughed while his family was dying that caused Dan to lower his shotgun. He slid the weapon onto a table.

He stood, feet apart, his fingers wet

with sweat. Every ounce of blood in his veins churned with anger and the need for vengeance. He was wrong to take this chance, but he couldn't help himself. Hearing that laugh, he had lost all reason.

Twelve years of grief forced his hand to his side.

Olson smiled. 'Say your prayers, Marshal.'

There was a long hesitation. Then Olson's eyes narrowed, his mouth twitching. A coolness settled over the man that was unmistakable. His vicious laughter still echoed in the room, even as he smiled.

Olson went for his gun.

Dan drew faster, his weapon leaping into his grasp and firing before Olson could pull the trigger. Dan's bullet slammed into Olson's forehead, right between the eyes. The shots were like thunder in the silence of the room.

Olson staggered backward, a crazed look on his face. He was dead before he hit the floor.

The gunman to Dan's left had drawn, but Hammer got him cold, a bullet slamming into the man's chest. The gunman on the right fired too, aiming right at Dan's head, but Tex Barker shot him from the stairs. Both gunmen dropped to the floor, dead.

Tex slowly came down the stairs, his six-gun still in his hand. He ran his fingers through his hair, then holstered his weapon.

Dan gazed at him with strange anxiety. He saw the slick black hair and mustache, the thin lips and dark eyes, the fancy clothes. How could this man be a Cassidy? Yet the way he walked, the way he smiled, all seemed to cry out that he was his father's brother.

Hammer came inside, and the big man checked the bodies. Other men and the bartender suddenly appeared. Wearily, Dan handed his shotgun to Hammer. Several of the onlookers were enlisted to carry the dead out of the room, and Hammer went with them.

Tex walked over to Dan. 'Can I buy

you a drink, Marshal?'

'No, I want to talk to you.'

'My office?'

'No, I haven't eaten. Let's go to the café.'

The gambler shrugged and put on his slicker and hat. The two men went outside side by side. Dan noticed that Tex's walk had a familiar swagger.

Dan had to know the truth about this man, before it was too late.

7

As he walked to the café with Tex
Barker, Dan could barely contain his
questions.

Tex was grumbling about the driving
rain and cold. 'Miserable night to go
out, Marshal. Besides, I don't eat out
much anymore. Got my own fixins.'

As they neared the café, Dan stopped
on the boardwalk, unable to make this a
friendly chat over a cup of coffee. He
turned, looked directly at the gambler,
and spoke gruffly.

'Miss Creighton told me you gave her
a story about the Cassidy murders.'

'That's right.'

'She says you're Tom Cassidy's
brother.'

'My real name is Tex Cassidy,
Marshal.'

'I've been told that Tom Cassidy had
light blue eyes and brown hair.'

129

'That's a fact. But you see, Marshal, my eyes are blue. If you look close, they're just mighty dark. My hair's brown, but I use a lot of grease on it. Fits my image. Seems I took after my grandfather, in more ways than one — he was hung as a horse thief.'

Dan swallowed, bending into the wind as he stared at this man. He remembered those stories about his great-grandfather. How much did this man really know?

'You see, Marshal, I was a bad one from the beginning. I got in scraps when I was too young to carry a gun. When I was fourteen, I had my first gunfight. I killed a man who was beating a woman with his six-gun. But witnesses lied and said it wasn't true, and his gun disappeared. They claimed he wasn't armed. The woman was too scared to testify because he had kin.

'I barely escaped being hanged. From that day forward, my family never answered my letters and refused to admit I existed, even though I heard years later that the sheriff pulled the warrant on me when he found out the witnesses had lied. By then, I was used to being Tex Barker, and it stuck.'

'You could be making this up.'

'Why should I? Listen, Marshal, I'm sticking my neck out by having my real name come out in the newspaper. Why would I do that if I weren't a Cassidy?'

'I haven't figured that out yet. Before I let her print that story, I want to be sure you're tellin' the truth.'

'And how can you do that?'

'I heard that Tom Cassidy had a long scar somewhere on his body.'

Hunched up in the rain, Barker nodded. 'Sure did, right across his back. From a rope burn. He got tangled up with a bronc we were trying to throw, and it cut right through his britches. He sure did yell. Is that the scar you mean?'

Dan nodded, his mouth so dry he couldn't speak. He just kept staring through the rain at this man. His uncle — Tex Cassidy. His heart was so full of joy he stood stock still in the rain with all of his strength washed away.

Drawing his slicker up to his chin, Tex looked irritated. 'Listen, Marshal, you've asked enough questions. Now you tell me how you knew about that scar. My brother wasn't one to brag on it.'

Dan felt his eyes burning, and he looked away.

'Marshal, you know somethin'. What is it?'

'I'm Tom Cassidy's son.'

There was a long awkward moment as they looked at each other, two lost souls who suddenly had found their past. Tex was so emotional he could hardly get his words out.

'You're Dan Cassidy?'

Dan nodded painfully. 'My little sister Ann died in my arms. When the back cellar door burned open, I crawled out. Shanks hid me, then sent me to Texas, where I changed my name.'

He drew a deep breath, then continued.

'Six months ago, I got a letter from Shanks telling me one of the killers had confessed. He was goin' to give me the names when I got here, but he was killed soon after he mailed the letter.'

Dumbfounded, Tex kept staring at Dan, who continued with difficulty, his voice barely audible. His heart was so full of agonized excitement, he had trouble finishing his story.

'With Shanks dead, the trail came to a halt.'

The two men stood gazing at each other, ignoring the driving rain running from their hats and the relentless wind. They were blood kin.

'You're my brother's son?' Tex murmured.

Dan nodded, his voice gone. Slowly, he lifted a hand to shake Tex's.

The gambler would have none of it. He reached for Dan and gave him a violent hug. The two men felt a joy they had never known, and their eyes were wet from more than the rain.

They drew away from each other,

staring each other up and down. His uncle gripped Dan's arm.

'You have my father's way of walkin',' Dan said. 'And you sound like him. And you even have the same nose and chin. I never realized it until tonight.'

'And you look a lot like him, Dan. I knew I liked you for some reason, but I couldn't put my finger on it. And look at you, a United States Deputy Marshal. My own nephew.'

Dan grinned. 'Well, Uncle Tex, I reckon it's time everyone knew who we were, but if we're both going to be targets, we'd better have a hearty last meal. But I got to know somethin'. Are your tables crooked?'

The gambler grinned back. 'I learned a long time ago that you don't need crooked tables to win. All the odds are with the house.'

Dan accepted his words as truth. 'By the way, I recognized Char Olson's laugh. He was at the ranch the night we were burned out.'

Tex's eyes brimmed. 'Well, he's gone now.'

The two men walked into the Four Star Café, where they sat at a corner table. Molly came over, her blue eyes sparkling. Tex stared at her, surprised and obviously taken by her smile and dimples.

'Molly's husband was the late sheriff,' Dan said.

'Yeah, I heard his widow was in town, but — '

Dan grinned at the way her gaze was fixed on Tex's stare, and he had to order for both of them. When Molly walked away, Tex swallowed hard.

'She's a beautiful woman.'

'You ought to eat out more, Tex.'

'You can bet on that. I'm not missin' a meal here.'

They spent the next two hours reminiscing about their family over supper. Tex talked about his childhood with his brother. Dan told of how he had learned to be a gunfighter from Shanks's cousin in Texas. His stories of his life as a town tamer sounded exciting, even to him. Tex told of his many years on the Mississippi, of gunfights over cards, his excitement obvious before he sobered.

'I came here five years ago when I learned of the murders, but I couldn't find out anything. But I figured with a federal badge here, it was my last chance to get someone to show his hand.'

'I don't like using the newspaper to do that,' Dan said. 'Why don't we just spread the word about who we are?'

'It'd take too long. And we're safer if the whole town knows at the same time. But listen here, Dan, you say you're twenty-seven. Why aren't you married, anyhow?'

'I never got over what happened. Women just reminded me of what I wanted to forget. But once it's settled, maybe I'll think about it. What about you and Laura Seton?'

'I was tryin' to get information from her, and it seems she was doing the same with you. Her pa probably wanted her to find out what you know.'

'She'll find out as soon as the story is printed. But I've got to find a safe place for Miss Creighton.'

'You like her, huh?'

Dan flushed. 'Maybe.'

'Well, the Setons have one good man, Carmody. Can you take him?'

'I'd hate to bet on it.'

Molly came to refill their cups; and Tex smiled at her. She smiled back, then hurried away. He tugged at his tie.

Dan leaned forward. 'Molly said she came here a few weeks ago. She was told that Shanks and her husband were both shot in the alley near your place.'

'Yeah, they were. But it was Saturday night both times. A lot of fools shootin' off their fire-arms in the street. No one paid much heed. Since there aren't any buildings behind my place, the killers got a clear ride out of town.'

They finished their meal and walked back into the heavy rain. They shook hands, firm and happy. Then his uncle hugged him again, squeezing the breath from him.

Dan watched the man walk away, bent to the wind. Then with a joy he hadn't known since he had first climbed into a saddle, he walked a little taller.

At the jail, he pounded on the door, and Hammer let him inside. Dan shook the rain from his hat and looked around.

'Where's Miss Creighton?'

'She went back to the newspaper office.'

'You let her go there alone?'

'Marshal, I just couldn't stop her.'

Dan nodded. 'I understand. I'll be back.'

Dan hurried across the street and down the boardwalk. Everyone was inside out of the storm, windows covered. Smoke from chimneys was dispersed by the downpour.

He was nearing the newspaper office when he saw flames pouring from open windows and sputtering under the roof overhang.

'No!' he cried.

And he ran through the mud like a wild man. The door was swollen and stuck, and he couldn't budge it. He used his six-gun to knock glass out of a window. He pulled his bandanna over his face and bravely leaped inside.

Hot fire licked at him, but his wet clothes protected him. Inside, nothing was burning except the walls and part of the roof. But the smoke was thick and choking.

He used the bar to force the door open. The new air made the fire flare up, but he had to be able to get out fast.

The heat was unbearable, the smoke blinding and burning his eyes. Dan staggered into the iron press. He got down on his knees, crawling beneath the smoke and reaching out crazily, unable to see anything.

He found something soft and frilly — a petticoat, then a slim ankle. He grabbed for Virginia and pulled her to him, lifting her to his chest. Fighting for breath in the heavy smoke, Dan rolled

Virginia into her slicker, which was lying nearby, and lifted her in his arms. She was so lifeless and limp, he was terrified.

With one mighty leap, he turned and rushed outside, coughing and falling to his knees as she fell from his arms onto the ground. His eyes burned so badly, he could barely see. He tried to get up, but he fell again, gasping for air.

Drawing on all his strength, despite the pain in his lungs, Dan lifted Virginia into his arms and charged across the muddy street toward the doctor's office.

He climbed the rickety stairs, fighting the wind until he reached the landing. He kicked hard at the door. The office was dark. Dan kicked again, nearly losing his balance. He was frightened, for Virginia looked so pale in his arms . . . just as his sister had.

'Don't die, Ann,' he had begged just twelve years ago, down in the hot, smoky cellar. His eyes stung now as he remembered, the pain shooting up through him, and he held Virginia tighter against him.

At last, lamplight came to the window. The door opened, and the doctor, dressed in his night-shirt, stood rubbing his eyes.

Dan carried her to the table and laid her down. 'Help her, Doc. I have to get back and make sure the fire doesn't spread.'

Dan paused only a moment to stare down at her still face. She didn't appear to be breathing.

Anguished, he spun on his heel and charged out of the office and back down the stairs. As he crossed the street in the rain, he saw that the fire was still contained in the newspaper office. Since no other buildings were connected, none were in any danger.

Dan stood near the hot fire, wondering if there were some way to save the press. Suddenly, part of the roof caved in, crashing down with a roar. Rain poured inside, drenching the smoke and flames. It wasn't long before the fire was nothing more than smoldering wood.

Dan moved in closer, seeing that the remaining roof had protected the press. Some of the type may have been damaged, but it looked as if even the newsprint stacked near the press had escaped the heat and flames.

He was glad for the rain, and grateful not everything had been lost. Satisfied the fire was out, Dan turned and slowly worked his way through the mud and back up the stairs.

The doctor let him in, and Dan hurried over to the long table where Virginia lay. Her eyes were open, but the whites had turned red. Her lips were parched and trembling. Dan was grateful that this time he had been able to save a life.

She lifted a weak hand. He grasped it and leaned close.

'Dan,' she whispered, 'what about the press?'

'It's all right. Do you know who did it?'

x

142

She shook her head. 'No. I was working. There was a knock at the door and someone called out. I thought it was you, so I opened it. Two men came in and started throwing the lamps around. When I fought and started to yell, they knocked me down. I guess I hit my head. But I scratched one of them on the neck when he put his hand over my mouth.'

'You didn't recognize them?'

'No. They had bandannas over their faces.'

Slowly, she closed her eyes, but held onto his hand as if it were the only way she could stay alive. Her skin was blistered, her lips so dry they were cracked.

'She'll have to stay here tonight,' the doctor said. 'She needs tendin'. You come back first thing in the mornin'.'

Dan reluctantly released her fingers. She didn't open her eyes, but she seemed to be breathing regularly. He turned and went back outside, the cold wind tearing at him.

He returned to the jail and slammed his fist down on his desk. He did not sleep well that night.

When Dan saw that first light was fighting through the dark storm, he took his slicker and walked to the doctor's office. The river was high and swollen, the water churning in dangerous-looking eddies. He decided to check the levee after he saw Virginia.

He found Virginia sitting up in a big chair, the doctor serving her coffee so thick it looked like mud. Her color had returned. A blanket was over her slim form. Molly was fussing over her.

When Virginia saw him, she smiled with relief. 'Oh, Dan, the doctor was telling me about Char Olson and those two men. I'm so glad you're all right.'

'Tex helped me.'

'Did you talk to him?'

'Yes, he's Tex Cassidy, all right. And I told him I was his nephew. And you can print that, right before I stick you in a cell.'

The doctor stared. 'You print your

real names as Cassidy, you'll both end up on boot hill.'

'Maybe.'

Virginia looked up. 'Dan, maybe it's not such a good idea.'

'Well, I agree with Tex. It's the only way we're ever going to find out the truth. We got to smoke 'em out.' He paused and looked sternly at Virginia. 'You stay here until I get back. I have to check the river. If it looks bad, I'll roust some of the men to hold the levee.'

'I'm going to my house, then.'

He tried to look mean. 'For once, will you do as I say?'

'But I have a home to worry about. And Molly's with me. Also, I want to look at the press. Besides, they know they've frightened me, and they think the press is ruined, so why should they bother with me now?'

Shaking his head, he knew he wasn't going to win. 'Please — stay here until Hammer comes to look after you.'

As he went outside, she called to him and followed and caught his arm. Her eyes were glistening.

'Wait, Dan. You saved my life. I didn't even thank you.'

Before he could resist, she was in his arms, sliding her hands up to his face. She reached upward, her lips beckoning, and he couldn't help himself. He bent his head and kissed her gently. She felt so small and vulnerable.

Slowly, she drew back and smiled. He swallowed hard, but the lump in his throat remained. Being near her was more than a man could stand without going crazy. He helped her back inside and quickly left.

When he got back to the jail, Tex was inside having coffee with Hammer. The two men seemed to have settled their differences.

Tex shook Dan's hand with a firm, happy grip. The man looked more like Dan's father every minute. Even his voice hit home.

'I just wanted to make sure I wasn't dreamin'. You are my nephew, sure as shootin'.'

'I'm glad you're here, Uncle Tex.'

Dan was grinning, but then he sobered and told them about the newspaper fire and the attempt to murder Virginia.

'All right,' Dan said. 'Now, one of you has to look after Miss Creighton. She's over at the doc's, but she's determined to go home.'

'Then let Hammer look after her,' Tex said. 'I'm goin' with you.'

Dan nodded and turned to Hammer. 'Don't you leave her side until I get back. Maybe they'll figure she's dead. And maybe with the building destroyed, they'll think she can't do more harm. Could be they'll leave her alone for now, but you watch out.'

Hammer nodded. 'Okay, Marshal.'

'And don't let her talk back to you,' Dan added.

Hammer looked so worried at this last remark that Dan had to reassure him. Then Tex and Dan headed back out into the storm. They could see lightning flashing on the far horizon.

They walked down toward the big livery and over to the bridge. Water was creeping up to the bank that had been built around the structure. If the earth gave way, the bridge could go, and the street would be flooded. Fortunately, it looked solid.

Suddenly, a deafening roll of thunder sounded across the northern sky, booming like an explosion and shaking the land.

'It's breaking up,' Tex said.

Sunlight appeared, even as it kept raining. But like magic, the storm slid across the sky toward the east, leaving patches of blue sky and, suddenly, a double rainbow in the west.

They stood on the boardwalk, staring at the sight.

'Dan, that's a sign for sure.'

They walked back in the remaining drizzle, Dan glancing at his uncle. 'As soon as the men who murdered our family are behind bars, I was figurin' on takin' my savings and finding a piece of land. Maybe raise horses.'

'You need a partner?'

Dan nodded with relief. 'I sure do.'

They paused to look at each other with pleasure. Tex put his hand on Dan's shoulder. 'Now that's settled, don't you let anything happen to you.'

'Same here. I been without kin too long.'

As they went toward the jail, they caught a glimpse of Hammer chasing Virginia across the street toward her newspaper office, so they laughed and followed.

The giant was now busy pushing the collapsed part of the roof aside as if it were kindling wood. As Dan and his uncle approached, it stopped raining.

Sunlight shone on Virginia's golden hair. She didn't see them and was busy looking in the wreckage. The front wall had crumbled down, but the interior seemed intact. They could see the hand press standing inside, untouched. Newsprint stacked next to it had only suffered smoke and water damage, and type had spilled.

Virginia was fussing over the trays of type that lined the walls. 'I don't see a decent R,' she said with a frown.

Then she turned and looked at Dan. She smiled in that way she had, reaching right inside his gut with a rush of warmth.

'Where's Molly?' Dan asked.

'She went to work.'

'Hammer's going to stay with you.'

She came over to him as she wiped soot from her hands. 'Dan, I'm worried. You and Tex will be targets. You'll just get killed. And then what? Nothing will have changed.'

For a long moment, he gazed at her, wanting to remember her just the way she looked right now: with ink on her chin, dust on her nose, that lovely smile on her face, and her flaxen hair falling free on her shoulders.

'We're doing what has to be done.' With that, Dan spun on his heel and went back up the street with Tex.

* * *

Meanwhile, the Setons were saddled up at their ranch. Giles was already on a big roan when Kirk and Karl dragged forward two men. One had scratches on his neck.

'Pa,' Kirk said, 'I just found out you sent these two mavericks to the newspaper office.'

'Sure, to destroy the press.'

'Maybe so, but they just told me they left Miss Creighton inside the burning building.'

Giles glared at the men. 'All right, speak up.'

The man with the scratches shook Kirk's hand from his arm. 'She went loco. I tried to shut her up. She fell and hit her head. We had to get out pronto.'

Kirk was furious. 'Listen here, fella, if she is dead, I'm comin' back here and wringin' your neck.'

'It was an accident, honest.'

'She see your faces?' he asked.

'No, we had 'em covered.'

Giles was grim. 'All right, we can't do anything about it now. And we're headed for town to take care of some business.'

Karl shoved the other man away from him and swung into the saddle. 'What about the marshal?'

'I ain't worried about Casey,' Giles said. 'He ain't bulletproof.'

Kirk shrugged. 'I'm beginnin' to think he is.'

'Well,' Karl said, 'we got Carmody, don't we?'

Kirk smiled, pulling his hat down tight. 'Don't worry, Pa. If Carmody can't take him, I can.' He drew his gun, spinning it like a showman.

'He's right, Pa. I seen Kirk practicing. He's faster'n lightning.'

'Takes more than speed to kill a

man,' Giles said. 'Ain't I taught you boys nothin'?'

Giles straightened in the saddle and headed toward town, his sons following. They had bought up mortgages on three small spreads surrounding their property, and now they were ready to foreclose. There was no doubt in Giles's mind he was going to own this valley, and no tin badge was going to stand in his way.

8

It was twilight when the Setons rode onto the bridge. The storm had been gone since noon. The waters had receded to some degree, and the bank was no longer in danger. It was cold and damp but windless.

Giles Seton rode between his two sons. They reined up near the livery and saw three men lounging farther down the east side of the street, one in front of the gambling hall and the others on a bench outside the Four Star Café.

'That's Carmody and his sidekicks,' Karl said.

Kirk grunted. 'They don't look so tough.'

'They're tough enough,' Giles said. 'And we can use 'em.'

The open doors to the livery were lit with lamps. As they dismounted, Dan and his uncle came forward from the shadows.

'Well, Marshal,' Giles said, 'you shouldn't surprise a man like that. Ain't safe.'

Dan moved closer, Tex away to his left.

'We're not lookin' for trouble,' Karl said. 'We're just spendin' the night in town. Over at my house. And I plan to visit Miss Creighton. Is she at the newspaper office?'

The Setons waited, holding their breath, and Dan obliged. 'There was a fire, but the place held up.'

'Was Miss Creighton hurt?' Karl persisted.

'She's all right.'

Karl swallowed hard, and Kirk looked relieved.

Dan studied them, reading them carefully. All three men seemed glad that Virginia was alive. Maybe they hadn't planned to murder her after all. But something else was afoot, all right. There was sweat on Kirk's nose. Karl's mouth was twitching. Giles was too calm for a man who could order death so easily.

Dan watched them lead their horses back to the stalls. Then he glanced at Tex, who had read them the same. They walked out into the last light of day.

Moving down the boardwalk, they came to a stop near Carmody, who smiled lazily, his dark eyes flashing. He was leaning on a post under the overhang.

'Good evening, Marshal.'

Dan nodded and walked on by with his uncle, heading back to the jail. They found Hammer and Virginia waiting inside.

'Here it is, Dan,' Virginia said, holding up the newspaper. 'I have a boy out there now, spreading it around.'

With Tex reading over his shoulder, Dan stared at the headlines as he took the paper in his hands:

CASSIDY FAMILY IN RAWHIDE

This editor has just learned that Tex Barker is none other than Tex Cassidy, brother of Tom Cassidy, who was murdered twelve years ago with his wife and child.

Even more surprising, it seems that United States Deputy Marshal Dan Casey is none other than Dan Cassidy, the sole survivor of those murders. It was a letter from Will Shanks that brought the marshal back to Rawhide.

Tex shrugged. 'Well, we wanted to get 'em out in the open. Now they'll come gunnin' for us for sure.'

But Dan wasn't convinced. 'Whoever killed our family isn't going to want their identity known. They'll come after us, but not in the open.'

'Yeah,' Tex agreed. 'Maybe you're right. Now what about Miss Creighton?'

'I'll be fine,' Virginia said. 'And Molly's staying with me. Besides, why would they harm me? It's you and your uncle they want.'

Tex agreed. 'She'll only get hurt if you keep her here, Dan.'

'Right now,' Dan said to Hammer, 'I want you spendin' the night up at the Creighton house and stayin' there 'til mornin'.'

* * *

Meanwhile, Giles Seton was in the near-empty Four Star Café with his sons. They were enjoying a hearty meal. Then a towheaded boy cheerfully sold them the day's newspaper.

When Giles saw the headlines, his face went red and he nearly choked on his food. 'Blast! Look at this!'

The three Setons crowded to read the newspaper in the light of the overhead lamp. Giles, his eyesight failing, had to peer close to the print, his anger rising.

Karl frowned. 'So Barker and the marshal are Cassidys. And the marshal was in that house we burned. Didn't seem like anyone could have survived. The roof had fallen in before we rode off.'

Giles leaned back. 'But they don't know we done it.'

'No, Pa,' Karl said. 'But we ain't never gonna rest easy 'til we get the Cassidys, once and for all.'

'They're sittin' over in that jail,' Kirk added. 'Maybe Tex will go back to his place tonight. We can get him in the open.'

'No,' Giles snapped, 'we'd give ourselves away. I'll think of somethin'. We ain't gonna hang, I know that.'

Karl lit his cigarette. 'We still got Carmody.'

Giles looked at his two sons. 'Listen to me, boys. All I want is this valley. We'll get rid of the Cassidys, one way or another, but we gotta be smart about it.'

Karl folded his arms. 'Then let's put Carmody on 'em, one at a time.'

Giles nodded, a smile slowly spreading across his face. 'Okay. But the marshal goes first.'

* * *

At the jail, the Cassidys had barred the door and settled down for the night. Dan had pinned a deputy's badge on Tex, who took it with good humor. Then there was a knock on the door. Dan peered through the window, seeing Hammer. He unbarred the door.

Behind Hammer were Virginia and Molly, carrying trays of food. Molly gave Tex a shy smile as she helped lay out the food on the table. There were cold cuts, hot beans, and hot bread.

'Now, we'll go home and feed Mr. Hammer,' Virginia said.

'You shouldn't be out at night,' Dan said.

She turned to look up at him. 'Do you know what your trouble is, Dan

Cassidy? You've forgotten how to say thank you.'

He swallowed, aching to kiss her, but terribly conscious of the onlookers. 'Thank you,' he said sheepishly.

Tex leaned on the desk, studying Molly, who studied him right back. 'Did you make the bread?'

'We both did,' Molly said. 'Don't forget to wash your hands before you eat.'

Tex laughed, and Dan let Hammer and the women out of the jail.

After eating the hearty supper, they took turns on guard that night, wondering what was going to happen. But the Setons were lounging comfortably at Karl's house, with word having been sent to Carmody.

The next afternoon, Carmody rode back into town with his two men, Mace and Buck. They were all ready for a fight.

They left their horses at the livery barn and headed toward the gambling hall, hoping to catch Tex by himself, but he wasn't there.

'Nope,' the barkeep said. 'He left me in charge. Took up a badge down there with his nephew at the jail.'

Carmody led the way back into the sunlight, but he paused in the street. 'Now, listen, both of you. This is my play. I'm takin' Dan Cassidy fair and square. You two just hang out in case he's got help. But there'll be no back shootin'.'

'Why do you care what happens?' Mace grunted.

'Yeah,' Buck cut in, 'what's so great about this here lawman?'

Carmody shrugged. 'He's the only man I ever respected.'

'So how you gonna handle it?' Mace asked, ignoring the profound thought. 'And what about Tex?'

'One at a time. Just go tell Dan I'm waitin'.'

'How you gonna make him draw?'

'Let me worry about that.'

Mace went down the street toward the jail, while Buck went back into the gambling hall. Carmody stood in the street, his shirt damp. He pulled his hat down tight on his brow, shading his eyes from the sun.

He was being paid a lot of money to kill Dan, enough to buy his own mountaintop, where he could lay his traps. Yet he knew there was no way he could quit this life. He had come too far.

Mace came out of the jail, both Cassidys following slowly, their badges gleaming in the sunlight. When Mace crossed the street to the other side, Tex turned to Dan.

'Let me take him, Dan. You got more life left to live.'

'I've seen you draw. I'm faster.'

'But we don't know how fast he is.'

Dan shrugged. 'I know. He saved my life once.'

'And that could slow your hand. Let me take him.'

'Tex, you stay back here in the shade.' Then Dan walked into the street.

He was conscious of faces at the windows, of men dodging into doorways. A woman pulled a child back into a store. There was a sudden stillness that pounded in Dan's ears.

He walked slowly, knowing Tex would keep an eye on Mace. But where was Buck?

Sweat on his back, Dan knew it would be a close call. Tex was right. Because Dan liked the man, it could slow his hand. His debt could make him hesitate.

He still remembered Carmody's words down in Texas: '*I don't like back shooters. A man's got a right to a fair fight, face-to-face, man to man.*'

And here Dan was facing Carmody, but he would try to avoid having to draw. Yet he knew all the games, and he feared that before this day was over, either he or Carmody would lie dead in the dust. He slowly moved forward.

Carmody stood tossing a silver dollar in his hand. 'I'm sorry about this, Dan.'

'Then turn around and head out.'

164

'I can't do that. I'm gettin' paid mighty well. And I got my reputation to keep.'

'What about that mountaintop?'

'It's too late for me, Dan.'

Righthanded, Carmody still carried a spare on his left. He moved easily, like a cat. Many men had lain dead at his feet over the years. He had taken them almost casually toward the end, but not now.

As Dan watched Carmody toss the coin over and over in his hand, he was suddenly conscious of Virginia running up the sidewalk to his right.

'Dan,' Virginia called, even as someone pulled her into a doorway. The echo of her voice rang in his ears.

Now he was within twenty feet of Carmody.

'You can still back off,' Dan said.

'I've seen you draw. I'm faster.'

'That was a long time ago. And I'm still younger.'

'Maybe. But when this coin hits the dirt, I'll have to kill you, Dan. Unless you're ready to turn tail and ride out.'

'Can't do that.'

So the two men drew a deep breath and prepared for one of them to die. Each had their lives flashing through their minds.

Carmody suddenly tossed the dollar high in the air. The silver glinted in the sunlight as the coin spiraled crazily downward.

When it hit the ground, both men would draw. Only one would be the winner.

9

The spiraling coin came crashing toward earth in the afternoon sunlight. Dan Cassidy and Carmody were facing each other, waiting for the moment when one would die.

From the jail, Tex had moved along the sidewalk, keeping his eye on Mace across the street. Buck was at the swinging doors of the gambling hall, watching with other curious men.

Virginia stood in the doorway of a store, crowding through several men to be able to see. She was pale and frightened.

And on the path coming down from the hillside near the river stood Kirk Seton. He had disobeyed his father, determined to be in on the kill, wanting to see Dan Cassidy hit the dirt. He moved along the boardwalk, pausing between the hardware store and the bakery.

The coin hit the dirt.

At the same time, both men drew, but Dan's Colt leaped into his hand a whistle faster. He fired just as Carmody pulled the trigger.

Carmody's shot burned Dan's left earlobe. Dan's shot hit Carmody square in the right shoulder, just where Dan had aimed.

Carmody staggered forward and dropped to his knees, his right arm dangling. He tried to draw the other gun with his left hand, but he fumbled, watching Dan approach, six-gun aimed at him.

'Drop it,' Dan said.

'Finish me, Dan. I'm no use to anyone now.'

'Listen to me, Carmody. I done you a favor.'

The gunman dropped his other Colt and gripped his right arm with his left hand. He staggered to his feet, blood running through his fingers. He stared at Dan, now understanding that Dan had purposely aimed at his shoulder.

'That was a rotten thing to do, Dan.'

'Now you can go find that mountain.'

Carmody swallowed hard, tears stinging his eyes. 'What good am I without my gun arm?'

'You can lay traps. And marry that girl.'

People were coming out on the street now, and Carmody felt embarrassed and foolish. Yet as he saw the doctor hurrying from the crowd, he hesitated long enough to turn to Dan, his voice low as pain shot through him.

'You done me wrong, Dan.'

Dan watched as Carmody turned away, the doctor leading him toward his office. He saw Tex coming into the street, his face flooded with relief. Dan turned to see Mace and Buck mingling with the crowd.

And he saw Virginia running toward him. She came to a halt a few feet away, out of breath. Tears were trickling down her cheeks and she was pale. As he slowly holstered his six-gun, she found her voice.

'Dan Cassidy, how could you take such a chance?'

Tex came to stand by his nephew. 'With Dan's speed, it wasn't much of one.'

She frowned and spun on her heel. She walked away with chin in the air, until she reached Molly on the boardwalk. Then she fell into Molly's arms, and the woman led her away.

Dan grinned. 'I guess she cares.'

'Listen, Dan, you had me plenty worried,' Tex said. 'I wasn't sure if your friendship was going to stop you.'

'I had to draw as soon as the coin hit. I had no choice. But I like Carmody, and I owed him. I wanted him to quit, once and for all.'

The men turned and walked back to the jail. Dan checked his revolver, reloading.

'I'm goin' to see Carmody. Hold down the fort, will you?'

'Just watch yourself.'

Dan continued up the street toward

the doctor's office. He climbed the stairs and knocked. The doctor let him inside, where Carmody was lying down with his right arm heavily bandaged.

Dan pulled up a chair and studied him. 'You look all right.'

'That was some shot. Fast as lightning. Beat me by a hair. And you were aimin' right at my shoulder?'

'I didn't want you dead.'

'I'm mad as the devil right now, and I got my regrets. But someday I'll thank you.'

'The Setons sent you, right?'

'Sure did. They said to call you out in a fair fight, that's all. They gave me five hundred, and I was to get another five hundred if I won.'

'Well, five hundred will take you a far piece.'

'You're right about the woman, Dan. I met her a year ago. Pretty as a Texas sunrise. Half Cheyenne and half angel. She's still waitin' up in western Montana.'

'Well, that's sure enough high country.'

'I'm leavin' Rawhide as soon as I can sit a saddle. Maybe tonight. Or I'll wait for the stage.'

Dan leaned back in the chair and loosened his bandanna. 'Well, you'd better marry that girl and find that mountain, or it'll all be wasted.'

'I never woulda quit, you know. But now, well, you gave me no choice, Dan.'

Dan shook his left hand and stood up with a grin. 'Maybe I envy you, Carmody.'

'You look me up someday. Ask for me at Butte. That's where I'll be pickin' up mail.'

Dan nodded and left the room. He felt good about Carmody. He had paid him back in a strange way, but the man would leave this way of life.

He walked back to the jail and spent the afternoon with Tex and Hammer.

Tex poured them all some coffee. 'Well, Dan beat Char Olson and now he's beat Carmody. So they'll have to

172

resort to ambush.'

'I saw Kirk Seton watchin' the whole thing,' Hammer said. 'He's sure a wild one.'

* * *

At the Seton ranch, Giles and Karl listened as Kirk related what had happened. Kirk was animated, hardly believing what he had witnessed.

The old rancher shook his head. 'That fast, eh?'

'But I can take him,' Kirk said.

'Don't talk foolishness,' his father replied. 'You done a lot of practicin', but out there in the street, it's a different story. Men like Cassidy and Carmody, that's their territory. Besides, I ain't about to lose a son.'

Karl leaned back in his chair, crossing one leg over his knee, his fingertips together. 'So what do we do now?'

'Everyone's been afraid of us up 'til now,' Kirk said. 'But now with two

badges in town, and Hammer backin'
'em up, some fool might know somethin' about the raid and speak up. We
ain't never gonna have no peace until
we're rid of every last Cassidy.'

'We still got Mace and Buck,' Karl
suggested. 'I believe they're still in
town.'

Giles nodded. 'Maybe we oughta
think about that. Kirk, you go in town
and find them two hard cases, but be
careful. Tell 'em to get out here so I can
talk to 'em.'

Later that night, Kirk Seton was in
the gambling hall, standing at the bar
and watching the men at the tables.
Faro and poker were going full speed.
There was a noisy roulette wheel, where
Josh Hartley was taking his chances.

Kirk stiffened. He hated the Hartleys.
And that Josh, dating Virginia Creighton and showing off his college
education. Well, Kirk had his own kind
of education, and he placed his hand on
his holster.

Kirk had already tossed back several

glasses of rye whiskey. His head was heavy, and he was feeling angry and spiteful. He had watched Dan Cassidy shoot down one of the fastest guns west of the Mississippi. The lawman had already taken Char Olson, who had been plenty fast, and now Carmody.

Angry that he didn't have enough guts to go down the street and call Cassidy out, Kirk was steaming. He had to prove he was more of a man than anybody.

He walked over to the table where Josh and two other men were betting on the spin of the wheel. He tossed his own coins onto the black. The wheel landed on red. Josh won double.

'Hartley, you're bad luck.'

Josh reddened, picked up his money, and went to a poker table. Soon Kirk followed and sat opposite him in a game where two grizzly miners were gambling their poke. A Hartley hired hand, aged and whiskered, watched and puffed on a pipe.

Hours passed. Josh was on a winning

streak, and money was piling up in front of him. The two miners finally cashed in and left, disgusted.

Now it was Josh and Kirk, playing hard and fast against each other. Men came to stand and watch. The bets were high, continuous, reckless.

Kirk had three tens. He raised the bet, and Josh called him. Kirk glared at the youth with his pink face and unbearable good manners. He spread out his hand, beaming with certainty.

But Josh had four queens. He reached to rake in the money. Kirk slammed his hand down on Josh's.

'Hold it. I saw that card up your sleeve.'

Josh turned red, withdrawing his bruised hand and staring at Kirk. The other men backed away hurriedly. The hall fell silent.

'What's that in your inside pocket?' Kirk demanded.

Josh pulled his jacket open and reached inside.

Kirk leaped to his feet and drew his

six-gun, firing so fast Josh didn't know what hit him. Blood spurted from his chest. His eyes went round as he slumped in his chair, staring at Kirk. He was clutching some papers in his hand.

Gunsmoke hung in the air. Kirk straightened, feeling like a man. He didn't hear the marshal and Tex enter the gambling hall from behind him.

Josh keeled over in the chair, the Hartley hand trying to hold him but finally realizing Josh was dead. The whiskered man gazed a long moment at the cocky Kirk, then turned and headed out of the gambling hall.

Coolly, Kirk turned and holstered his six-gun, his chin in the air, showing the whole room he was a fast gun. But then he paused, staring at the barrel of Dan's shotgun.

'Kirk Seton, you're under arrest.'

'For what? He drew first.'

But Tex, kneeling by Josh, looked up. 'He's unarmed.'

There was such a hush in the room that Kirk could hear his own heart rattling in his chest. He couldn't breathe. He wanted to yell for his father and brother. He wanted to shout he was a Seton and no one could aim a shotgun at his belly.

He looked over at Buck, who was half-drunk but watchful. Buck would go to the ranch and tell what happened. The Hartley cowhand had already left. The man would run and tell Judson and Jed Hartley about Josh's death.

Sweat formed on Kirk's ruddy face. His mustache twitched. And the shotgun was still aimed at his belly.

'Let's go,' Dan said.

'You got it in for us Setons.'

'You shot an unarmed man.'

'You're lyin'.'

Tex had the two miners look at Josh's body, and the men confirmed there was no weapon. They stood up, shaking their heads.

Kirk's face was as red as his

mustache. He couldn't move as Tex came from behind and took his Colt as well as the knife in his boot. He felt naked, angry.

'My pa will get me out.'

'Not 'til the circuit judge gets here,' Dan said.

'When will that be?'

'Wednesday,' Tex said. 'Always the second Wednesday of the month, and that's the day after tomorrow.'

'You're crazy. I ain't rottin' in jail for two days for a lousy mistake. I thought he was pullin' a gun. Everyone will tell you that.'

'Tell it to the judge.'

Kirk was furious yet helpless. He let himself be marched out the door but nodded to Buck, who was ready to leave. It was dark and cold outside. The stars and moon were hidden by heavy clouds. The air was damp.

They crossed the street and headed down to the jail. Inside, the lamps were still burning. Hammer wasn't there, as

Dan had insisted he spend every night at Virginia's. But they would be needing him.

Kirk was half intoxicated, staggering and snorting his anger even as they shoved him in a cell.

'My pa's gonna hang you for this,' he yelled.

'Maybe we oughta hang him,' Tex said. 'Seems to me you Setons had a hand in what happened to the Cassidys.'

'I don't know nothin' about that.'

'You were old enough to have gone on the raid.'

'Get away from me.'

'Maybe we won't have to do nothin',' Tex said. 'Seems to me Josh has a couple of mean brothers.'

Kirk tried to remain cocky, but his eyes were wild. 'I ain't scared of no Hartleys.' He turned his back and sat down on the cot. He was dazed from the whiskey, fearful of the Hartleys, worried his father and brother wouldn't come. But soon the liquor kicked in and he was fast asleep.

Tex closed the door to the cell area and pulled up a chair near the stove. 'Well, now that we got the devil in jail,' he said, 'what are we going to do?'

'I don't know. The Setons aren't going to be quiet for two days, that's for sure.'

'And the Hartleys are going to be plenty hot about this.'

Dan leaned back in his chair. 'I'd hate to count the number of guns that are going to be aimed at this jail — Hartleys tryin' to kill him. Setons tryin' to save him.'

'Maybe we ought to get Kirk out of town.'

'We'd be trailed and gunned down in the open.'

'So we board up here. We'll need supplies. You sit tight, Dan. I'll get us fixed up. And I'll get Hammer.'

Dan agreed, and Tex went out into the night. Dan checked his six-gun, his fingers cold. The Hartley ranch was closer than the Setons', and the two brothers would ride all night to get here.

Come morning, Rawhide was going to explode.

10

It was drizzling when Tex reached Virginia's house that night. A lamp burned at the front window. He pounded on the door, and Hammer peered out through the curtains. He opened the door.

'What's happenin', Tex?'

'Get your boots on. We got trouble.'

A light appeared from the stairs, and the two women came down in their dressing gowns. Virginia hurried forward, looking anxious, Molly at her heels.

'Tex, what's wrong?'

'Well, you'll hear about it anyway. Kirk Seton gunned down Josh Hartley at the gambling hall. Accused him of cheating. But Josh wasn't armed.'

Virginia put a hand to her throat. 'Oh, no. Is Josh — '

'He's dead, all right. We got Kirk in jail.'

Hammer sat down to pull on his boots, but he was shaking his head. 'Them Hartleys will sure be mad.'

'And the Setons,' Virginia said.

Molly stood beside Virginia, her red hair long and soft on her shoulders. To Tex, Molly was more beautiful than any woman he had ever met. He felt awkward in front of her.

'Tex,' she said, 'can't you get Kirk out of town?'

'No, but we'll board up in the jail.'

Virginia was frantic. 'I have to see Dan.'

'You're stayin' right here, and keeping your doors locked. Hammer's goin' with us. We figure they don't care about the newspaper much now, so you'll be safe.'

Hammer went outside, and Tex was about to follow, but he paused, looking at the women in the lamplight.

'Don't worry,' he said.

But as he closed the door behind him, he knew his words wouldn't stop them from pacing the floor all night. He felt warm inside, knowing Molly might be thinking about him.

He and Hammer went back down to the main street and the general store, collecting supplies and ammunition. They returned to the jail, and Dan let them inside.

'We'd better try to get some sleep,' he said.

'I've had several hours,' Hammer said. 'You two go ahead.'

But Dan and Tex had trouble sleeping, knowing that trouble was coming. Sure enough, they were startled out of their cots by a violent knocking at the door. Dan peered out a window behind the wooden shutter, seeing the rain and first light of day and two Hartleys pounding furiously.

'Open up, Cassidy,' Judson Hartley yelled.

Taking the shotgun, Hammer went into the cell area, closing the door behind him. Dan drew his six-gun and had it ready as he opened the door. Tex was seated at the desk, rifle across his knees.

Judson and Jed Hartley charged inside. Their lean faces and big jaws were set with fury. They stood in the middle of the room as Dan closed the door behind them.

'Where is he?' Judson demanded.

'Who?'

'Don't pull that on me, Marshal. Where's Kirk Seton?'

'We're holding him for trial. The judge will be here tomorrow on the stage.'

'Trial, huh. We'll see about that. I wanta talk to him,' Judson persisted.

'He's asleep, and you're leaving.'

Judson looked from Dan's steady six-gun to Tex's rifle. He studied the closed door to the cells, his face dark with color.

'Where's Hammer?' Jed grunted.

Dan nodded to the back door to the cells. 'He's in there, with a shotgun.'

186

'All right,' Judson said, 'but we'll be back.'

'The door won't be open.'

'Then we'll have to open it.'

The Hartleys stormed back outside, and Dan barred the door behind them. He holstered his six-gun and breathed with relief. Tex shook his head.

'Dan, we sure got trouble here.'

'If the Hartleys are smart,' Dan added, 'they'll act now, before the Setons ever show.'

Hammer came out of the back room, curious.

'Hammer,' Dan said, 'I think you'd better take up residence back there.'

★　★　★

While the men in the jail made plans, the two Hartley brothers were standing in the rain.

'We'll never blast 'em out,' Jed said.

'We gotta have a trade.'

'You thinkin' what I'm thinkin'?'

'Yeah, and I know where she lives.'

187

'But we ain't gonna hurt her,' Jed growled.

'No, but the marshal don't know that. All we want is Kirk.'

The Hartleys mounted and rode through the alley and up toward the Creighton house. It was barely light. They saw a lamp burning in one of the upstairs windows as they dismounted. There was an outside stairway to the veranda, and both men climbed it as quietly as they could, the rain hiding any sound of their steps.

Peering in the lit, open window, they saw Virginia. She had her riding skirt on and was buttoning her jacket. She was wearing boots. As she reached for her slicker, Judson charged through the window.

Virginia spun around. Then she reached wildly for a six-gun that hung on the wall near her bed. Judson grabbed her arm, jerking her around. He slapped her hard.

'Now you be quiet, or the other woman will get hurt.'

'What do you want?' she demanded.

'They got Kirk Seton in jail. We're tradin' you.'

'They won't do it.'

'They'd better. Now come on.'

Judson draped her slicker around her, then dragged her to the window and shoved her outside. She fell into Jed's arms, and they marched her down the stairs.

They lifted her roughly onto Jed's horse, her feet dangling on the left side, and Jed sat behind her. Judson mounted his own horse and led the way back down the hill in the rain.

In front of the jail, Judson dismounted and pounded on the door. 'Open up, Cassidy. We gotta trade.'

Dan peered out through the window. He was startled to see Virginia mounted in front of Jed, the man's big arm tight around her and his sixgun pointed at her head.

Grimly, he pulled on his hat and opened the door, waving Tex to stay inside. He walked out onto the porch, his heart pounding at the sight of the gun barrel pressed to Virginia's temple.

Judson stood six feet clear of Dan. 'All right, Marshal. This is it. We turn her loose if you give us Seton.'

'And if not?'

'We'll take her out to the ranch or somewhere else. You may never see her again.'

'Go ahead.'

'Well, maybe we'll just kill her right here and get it over with. Jed, you got an itchy finger?'

'I sure do. I'll put a hole right through her if you don't give us Seton, Marshal.'

'What'll you do with him?'

'Hang him,' Judson said.

'The law will do that anyway.'

'We ain't takin' no chances. Them Setons are as slippery as greased pigs.'

Dan looked casual. 'You hang Kirk, I gotta hang you.'

'No jury would convict us. Josh wasn't armed,' Jed said.

'We're waitin' for the judge.'

Jed sneered. 'I'll blow her head off.'

Dan had sweat on his face. His instincts told him that these men were not women killers. But they were as mad as wet hornets. He had to do something, and he had to do it fast.

His hand moved near his holster. He saw Judson sneer.

Just then Virginia dug her boots into Jed's horse and kicked violently. The animal reared. Jed reached for the reins, leaving her hands free. She grabbed his gun hand, sinking her teeth into his wrist. Jed yelled, jerking the reins. His horse reared and spun.

Virginia kicked and fought. Both she and Jed were suddenly thrown by the frightened horse as it bucked. They landed sprawled in the mud. Judson stared, then turned to look down the barrel of Dan's six-gun.

His horse running away, Jed had fallen facedown in the mud. He was fighting to clear his eyes as he got to his knees. Virginia had retrieved his six-gun. She stumbled to her feet and aimed Jed's gun at him as he stood up and staggered backward.

'Don't move,' she said.

Tex came onto the porch, rifle ready. 'What now, Dan?'

Dan was stymied. If he locked them up, they'd tear down the bars trying to get to Kirk. If he let them go, they'd hire some gun hands and return to blast the lawmen out of the jail. And about that time, the Setons would arrive.

Judson was furious about the turn of events. 'Yeah, Marshal, what are you gonna do now?'

'You got any suggestions?'

'Give us Kirk.'

'No.'

'You gonna lock us up?'

'I'm thinking.'

'Lock 'em up,' Tex said. 'Hammer will be back there with the shotgun.'

Dan hesitated, but he knew he couldn't sit around and wait for the Hartleys to break down the jail. He'd feel better if they were out of his hair.

Dan marched Jed and Judson back to the jail, where two cells stood empty between them and the nervous Kirk. He pointed the Hartleys toward the end cell.

'What's goin' on?' he demanded.

'These two men want to hang you,' Dan said, locking the door on the Hartleys. 'So if I were you, I'd be good and quiet and sit right there in your corner.'

'It was a lousy mistake,' Kirk called to the Hartleys. 'I thought he was goin' for his gun. There's witnesses.'

'My brother didn't carry a gun,' Judson snarled.

'You're gonna hang,' Jed added.

Dan pointed to the corner behind Kirk. 'Like I said, go sit down and be quiet.'

Hammer remained in the back with his shotgun, and Dan returned to the front, closing the door behind him. Tex barred the door.

Virginia sat by the wood stove,

shivering. She still held Jed's gun. She looked up at Dan, her face void of color.

'Dan, would Jed have shot me?' Her eyes were wide with question, as if wondering why Dan had been so casual.

Tex intervened. 'Any move, and Jed would have killed you for sure. Dan was bluffing them, but he was getting ready to take a chance.'

Dan nodded. Weary, he sat down at his desk, his face in his hands. He shuddered down to his boots. The thought of Virginia dying as he watched had left him drained.

Tex stood up. 'I'll take a look around outside.'

When Dan didn't answer, Tex nodded to Virginia to bar the door behind him. She obeyed and turned to see Dan still with his face in his hands, his elbows on the desk.

She walked over and put her hand on his shoulder, feeling him tremble at her touch. He turned and looked up, seeing her lovely face. Her soft hand remained on his big shoulder.

'Dan, I'm sorry.'

'You were plenty brave, fighting yourself free.'

Slowly, he stood up, his arms went around her, drawing her tight against him. She rested her face on his chest, and he held her a long moment.

Then she leaned back and gazed up at him, her lips moist and parted. He bent his head and kissed her gently. She kissed him back. It was a warm, tender moment.

'You gave me a bad scare,' he muttered.

Just then there was a pounding at the door.

'Dan, let me in!' Tex yelled.

Releasing Virginia, Dan went to open the door and let his uncle inside. Tex was quick to replace the bar.

'Dan, the Setons are comin' in with a passel of men.'

'We've got to get Virginia out of here.'

She stood as tall as possible. 'I'm staying.'

'Well,' Tex said, 'we can't do nothin' right now, except tell Seton to back off while she's here.'

'I'm goin' outside,' Dan said. 'You cover me from the window. And Virginia, you come with me. I'm gettin' you on your way.'

'But they won't attack if I'm here.'

Dan made a face. 'Don't believe it. Come on.'

He seized her wrist and marched her outside onto the porch under the roof overhang. The Setons were riding up the street with a dozen gunmen, including Mace and Buck. Giles and Karl Seton rode forward.

Karl looked surprised. 'Virginia, what are you doing here?'

'The Hartleys tried to trade me for your brother.'

'Where are the Hartleys?' Giles demanded.

'In jail,' Dan replied.

196

Karl rode forward. 'Virginia, let me ride you home.'

Giles was annoyed. 'What about your brother?'

'I'll be right back,' Karl snapped.

Virginia hesitated, glancing at Dan.

'Take Judson's horse,' he suggested.

She smiled with relief and walked over to the hitching rail, where Judson's bay was still tied. She mounted and rode away alone in the rain. Dan was glad to see her away from the jail, and he looked up at Giles, who had seen Tex's rifle in the window. Dan spoke clearly.

'You got no business here.'

'I want to see my son.'

'All right, but just you.'

Giles followed Dan inside, and Tex barred the door. They took Giles's side arm. For a long moment, Giles looked over the room, studying it. He saw the well-shuttered windows, the rifle slots in the walls. It had the look of a fortress. He shrugged and followed Dan through the back door.

Kirk was asleep in the first cell, and in the third cell in the back, Giles saw the leering Hartleys. He also saw Hammer seated at the left wall with a shotgun.

'Giles, you listen to me,' Judson said. 'Your boy's gonna hang.'

Giles ignored him and turned to Dan. 'Let me in with my son.'

Dan checked in his boots and under his coat to be sure he had no knife or Derringer. Then he opened the cell and let Giles inside. The rancher walked over to sit on his son's cot and shake him awake.

Kirk looked up, startled.

'Are you all right, son?'

'Pa, I thought he had a gun.'

'I know, son. They can't hang you for that.'

'But you gotta get me out of here, Pa.'

'I'm workin' on it.'

Giles stood up and saw that there were only two small, high windows near the ceiling in the first and third cell, and no back door. Frowning, he went to the cell door, and Dan let him out.

'What about bail, Marshal?'

'No judge here to set it.'

'I give you my word that he'll be here for trial.'

'Sorry.'

Giles was fuming. 'Then whatever happens is on your head, Marshal.'

'I might make a trade.'

'And what's that?'

'The Cassidy killers for your son's bail.'

Giles's jutting jaw trembled. 'Get out of my way.'

Dan moved aside and followed the furious rancher into the front office. Tex unbarred the front door.

Giles paused before walking outside. He glared at Dan and Tex, then looked around the room again. He had a fix on everything, and his eyes were gleaming. Then he stormed outside, Dan closing and barring the door behind him.

'We're in some mess,' Tex said.

They went to the stove and sat down,

gazing at each other. Suddenly, they both grinned.

'At least we're in this together,' Tex said.

'They're gonna hit us hard.'

'With what? These walls are pretty thick.'

'Dynamite.'

'Well, maybe. They wouldn't want to kill Kirk, so they'd have to know what they were doing.'

'We'd better move our bunks out into the cell area.'

'You know, Dan, this is gettin' out of hand. We came here to find the men who killed our family. And here we are protectin' a man who could be one of 'em.'

'I know.'

'So what are we gonna do?'

'I'm still wearin' a badge, and so are you.'

'I took this tin star to help you.'

'And?'

Tex grinned uneasily. 'Well, I reckon if we're ever gonna see that horse ranch, we'd better start movin' to the back of this place.'

Dan nodded, his mind working. Somehow they had to get out of this trap. Nothing was going to hold this town together until the judge arrived. They had one night to go.

By that time, they could all be dead.

11

It was late afternoon on Tuesday, and the Setons were at the Four Star Café, trying to work things out. They were the only customers.

'Mace got the dynamite,' Karl said, his voice low.

Giles leaned close over the table. 'We'll blast open the front just enough to get the Cassidys and leave the back still standing so Kirk won't be hurt. We'll send the men inside to get rid of Hammer.'

'We could be hanged for this.'

'And who's gonna arrest us? Both Cassidys will be dead. And there ain't no one in this town with guts enough to testify against us.'

Karl sipped his coffee. 'What about the Hartleys? They're pretty mad. They might blab to the law about what happened twelve years ago.'

'And get themselves hanged? Not likely.'

'Maybe you're right, Pa. But with Olson dead, there's only two other men in this town who know we led the Cassidy raid, and that's the Hartley boys.'

Giles nodded. 'So we'd better make a clean sweep.'

'First we gotta get Kirk out.'

'That fool kid. Had to show he was a man.'

'But he's nearly thirty-three, Pa. He's not a kid. And he rode with us that night. The Hartleys were the youngsters. But none of us were kids when we rode away from the Cassidy spread.'

Giles sipped his coffee, savoring the taste. He looked at his son the banker and thought of his other son, the gunman. He had always been proud of them, but now he was worried. He felt his world slipping away.

★ ★ ★

While Giles and Karl made plans, Kirk lay on the cot in his cell watching patiently as Hammer awakened from a snooze across the room.

'How about some coffee?' Kirk demanded.

'Don't mind if I do. But you can just wait for supper.'

The big man strolled out of the room and through the door to the front office. The door closed behind him with a slam, leaving the prisoners alone.

Kirk stood up, grabbing the bars.

'Listen here, Judson, we gotta talk.'

The older Hartley stood up first, then Jed followed. The two men came to the bars and looked through the empty center cell between them and Kirk. Their anger had become bitter.

'What do you want, Seton?' Judson snapped.

'Look, we've spent a lot of time together.'

'You killed our baby brother.'

'It was an accident.'

'We'll see you hang.'

'If I hang, I'm takin' you both with me.'

'That so?' Judson growled. 'Then your pa and brother will hang right along with us. They were on that raid just like us. And you.'

Jed nodded. 'And we got caught up in it, if you remember, Kirk. I was only fifteen, and Jud was seventeen. We thought we was just there to scare 'em out. It was you Setons who got out of hand and left us with nightmares we ain't never gonna forget.'

'This ain't gettin' us anywhere,' Kirk said.

'That's right,' Judson said.

'My pa will be bustin' me out of here. Maybe he'd let you out if you was to back off.'

'How's he gonna get in? This place is a fortress.'

'He'll blast 'em out, that's what.'

'Dynamite? He'll kill us all.'

'No, because I figure they'll get Mace, since he knows all about it. He'll just blow the front and get the

Cassidys. Then we'll all be out, and there won't be nobody to point the finger at us. We're in this together.'

'Maybe,' Jed said, 'but we didn't kill old Shanks, or the sheriff, or Creighton.'

Kirk grimaced. 'Neither did I.'

There was a long silence. Finally Jed mumbled something to his brother, who mumbled back. He straightened.

'We'll think on it.'

Relieved, Kirk returned to his cot. He watched the brothers sit back down, just as Hammer reentered carrying his cup of coffee.

In the front, the Cassidys opened the door for Molly and Virginia, who had brought supper. The prisoners' food was delivered to Hammer along with his own meal, then Dan and Tex hurriedly sat down to roast beef and apple pie. They were ravenously hungry.

Molly and Virginia watched, pleased.

'Well,' Molly said, 'I can see we're not needed around here.'

His mouth full of hot roast beef and

mashed potatoes, Tex looked up, startled, as if he had forgotten they were there. Both men suddenly looked sheepish. The women smiled.

Dan swallowed. 'Thank you for bringing the food. It's right delicious.'

'Outstanding,' Tex managed.

Dan stood up, glancing at Virginia, so lovely in a blue dress. Her hair was loose on her shoulders, and there was white lace at her throat and wrists. Her dark blue eyes were shining.

'Well,' Dan said, 'won't you ladies sit down?'

'We think we should stay with you,' Virginia said. 'Maybe they won't bother you then.'

Tex sipped the hot coffee they had brought. It was clear and tasty, not like the hot mud on the stove. He glanced at Molly, her red hair pulled back from her face, dimples flashing.

'Sorry,' Dan said, 'but you both had better leave.'

'I'll see 'em home,' Tex offered.

Virginia shook her head. 'It's raining,

but it's still daylight, and we'll be fine. Besides, the Setons would just love to catch one of you out in the open. Anyway, we're armed.'

The men were startled as Molly reached inside her slicker and showed the six-gun stuck in a sash at her waist. Molly had a Derringer in her purse, which dangled from her arm.

'I'll send Hammer with you,' Dan said.

Virginia shook her head. 'Don't worry. The doctor sent two men to stay in our living room. They're waiting across the street.'

Tex frowned. 'What men?'

Virginia laughed. 'Two men who are at least seventy, but they have rifles. The Corley brothers. By the way, we saw the Setons through the window at the café. And that Mace was with them.'

The men walked to the door with Virginia and Molly. As Dan removed the bar, he looked down at Virginia. How he longed to pull her into his arms. She smiled up at him and went outside. Molly glanced at Tex, then she followed.

'They'll be all right,' Tex assured Dan. 'I know the Corley brothers. They can slice an apple at ninety feet.'

'All right, then. I guess we'd better finish supper before it gets cold.'

They dove into the plates of delicious food. When they had finished, they leaned back in their chairs and looked toward the shelves where their own food supply was stored. It was going to be a long night before the circuit judge came.

* * *

Over at the café, the Setons were discussing their plan with Mace. They didn't much like the ugly man, but they needed him. He had used dynamite in the mines down in Arizona. He knew how to lay a fuse without blowing himself up.

'Make it around two in the mornin',' Giles said.

'Buck will be here to help,' Mace told them.

Karl shook his head. 'I don't trust him.'

Mace grunted. 'You get what you pay for.'

'Never mind,' Giles cut in. 'We're payin' you plenty for this, so if you get caught, you better not say who sent you.'

'We ain't gonna get caught,' Mace said.

The men continued their plans while the Cassidys made their own. The Setons went up to Karl's house. And around two in the morning, Mace and Buck began to make their move.

The rain made the night dark and miserable, but it was good cover. Mace handled the dynamite, while Buck acted as lookout, kneeling down behind the trough in front of the smithy. There was no one on the street.

The jail looked quiet. They could see the lamplight through the cracks in the windows and rifle slits in the walls.

They figured at least one Cassidy was asleep.

Mace played it smart. He wanted the fuse to burn away from the rain, so he stayed under the roof overhang and knelt. He laid the sticks of dynamite under the windows and in front of the door, stringing the fuses along the wall. At the edge of the wall, he struck a match.

Suddenly, the barrel of a six-gun pushed hard against his ear. He froze, the match burning slowly toward his fingers.

'Put it out,' Dan said.

Mace threw the match into the rain. He slowly got to his feet, and he could feel Dan taking his six-gun. His ugly face twisted with fury. Now his hands were being cuffed behind his back, and he was spun around.

He saw Buck being pushed forward by Tex. The lawmen had slipped out unseen and had hidden in the smithy, just waiting for them. Buck was so angry he nearly exploded.

'Get movin',' Dan ordered both prisoners.

Tex carefully retrieved the dynamite and fuses, then followed the others inside, where the lamps were burning low. He placed the explosives on the table, then helped Dan prod the two gunmen into the back, where Hammer put them in the center cell.

The other prisoners were asleep until the cell door clanged as it was locked. They sat up, rubbing their eyes and staring at their new cellmates.

Mace was furious. 'You can't keep us in here. We didn't do nothin'.'

Dan and Tex ignored them. They grinned at Hammer, who grinned back.

'We'll spell you later,' Dan said.

'Just let me get some coffee.'

When the three lawmen went up front, Mace turned to glare at Kirk. 'You got us into this. Now get us out.'

Kirk was nervous. 'Where's Pa?'

'He's up at Karl's house. We was goin' to dynamite the front of the jail.

They was waiting for us.'

'Kirk,' Judson said, 'your pa better find some other way to get us out. If this keeps up, there won't be no room in here, and I sure don't like the smell now.'

Mace turned on him, snarling through the bars.

'Somethin' better happen,' Jed agreed. 'The stage comes in before noon, and the judge will be on it. And I hear he's a hangin' judge.'

It was then that Hammer returned with his coffee, and they fell silent, anger simmering as they wondered how they were going to escape.

Up front, the Cassidys sat down at the table and stared at the dynamite.

'What are we goin' to do with it?' Tex asked.

'Can't do much in town. You know anything about it?'

'No, but Hammer probably does. He worked a mine.'

'Well, we won't need it,' Dan said. 'The judge will be here before noon.'

'What do you figure the Setons will do?'

'Well, they don't want Kirk dead, that's for sure.'

The two men took turns sleeping. In the morning, when daylight peeked through the window, they were glad to see that the rain had stopped.

They heard thunder. It sounded like the heavy rumble of hoofbeats and the wheels of the stage, soon to arrive. It was time for Rawhide to be put to the test.

12

On Wednesday morning, the Setons and their men took up stations along the street. The gray clouds were moving across the blue of the sky, and the sun was shining. A rainbow arched in the distance.

The stage reached the town in mid afternoon. On board were five miners ready to try their luck. The remaining passenger stepped onto the boardwalk in front of the store near the jail.

Stocky and short, with white hair and a top hat, his black coat flowing about him, the judge looked more like a messenger of death. He had a crooked nose and white mustache. His gray eyes scanned the town.

Dan came to meet him. 'Glad to see you, Judge.'

'Casey? What are you doing here?'

'Let's talk.'

The judge went into the jail. Dan paused, seeing Carmody coming to the stage, his good arm carrying his gear, his horse trailing. The driver tied the animal behind the stage and threw Carmody's gear on top. The gunman's right arm was in a heavy sling. Turning slowly, Carmody forced a smile and waved good-bye. He climbed aboard and the stage rumbled off.

Dan and Tex spent the next hour filling in the judge on the events in Rawhide. The judge sipped the harsh black coffee and shook his head.

'What are you plannin' to do about the Setons?'

Dan shrugged. 'Well, I know they killed our family. I just can't prove it.'

'And the Hartleys?'

'They may have been in on it, but they're not killers, just hotheaded.'

Tex agreed. 'They don't like the Setons much.'

'Then maybe,' the judge said, 'they'd take immunity for testifyin' against the Setons.'

'They have their own code of honor,' Dan said, doubtful.

'But they don't want to hang,' the judge argued.

'Let's get 'em up here,' Tex suggested.

Dan called to Hammer to bring in the Hartleys. A moment later they appeared, their hands cuffed behind their backs. They looked disgruntled.

'The judge wants to talk to you,' Dan said.

The two men glared at the judge sitting at Dan's desk, but they were silent and listened as he spoke.

'If you men were on the Cassidy raid, you could get immunity by testifying against the Setons. I'd also consider dismissal of the charges of kidnapping a woman and threatening her life.'

'You got nothin' on us about no murders,' Judson said with a grunt.

'That's true, but you'd better think about it,' the judge said, his mustache twitching.

The Hartleys were taken back to

their cells. Dan and Tex opened the shutters to peer outside at the sunshine.

'We'll set up the court in the gambling hall as usual,' Tex said.

And so a few hours later Tex, Dan, and Hammer, along with the grizzled Corley brothers, marched all the prisoners across the muddy street and up to the gambling hall.

Laura Seton was waiting outside, her face pale. She looked frightened and signaled to Dan, but he ignored her and went inside with the others. He looked back to see her joining her father and brother in the back row of the hall.

The citizens of Rawhide crowded inside to watch the proceedings. Virginia and Molly were seated across from the Setons and their dozen gunmen. A jury of merchants, cowmen, and miners was sworn in and seated to the left of the judge, who was at a desk facing the courtroom and the prisoners.

Dan acted as prosecutor. John Beeker, the portly merchant who had some legal knowledge, had volunteered to defend all the prisoners.

Mace and Buck were charged with malicious mischief and attempted murder and were tried first. Their plea was not guilty. They would not tell who had hired them, despite intense questioning by Dan. They were sentenced to five years at Canon City State Prison. The looks on their faces as they were moved to the back of the room were not lost on the Setons.

The Hartleys were brought in front of the judge next and were charged with attempting to break into the jail and remove a prisoner. They were also charged with transporting a woman against her will and with assault and battery.

'If you men remember our discussion at the jail,' the judge said, 'then stand aside.'

The Hartleys returned to their chairs, and it was Kirk Seton who faced the judge. He pleaded not guilty to charges of manslaughter and murder. Witnesses testified that Kirk had made a mistake.

They, too, had thought Josh was going to draw his gun. The jury nodded, sympathetic.

Abruptly, Judson Hartley stood up. 'Judge, I got something to say.'

Judson was sworn in, his face pale, his eyes gleaming. 'My brother Josh was just a boy, an Easterner,' he said. 'Everyone in this town knows he didn't carry a gun. And so did Kirk Seton.'

The jury listened but didn't appear swayed.

Judson returned to his chair. He and his brother mumbled to each other. Then Jed stood up, his shoulders back.

'Your Honor, we got somethin' else to say.'

'I protest,' Beeker said. 'Your Honor, these men want Kirk Seton to hang, and they'll say anything to see it happen.'

But Jed was allowed to take the witness chair next to the desk, and he was sworn in, his face solemn. His gaze went directly at Kirk, then to the back

220

of the room where the Setons were watching.

'Your Honor, me and Judson was boys just twelve years ago. We was on that Cassidy raid, sure, but we thought it was for a lark. Kirk and Karl there, and their old man, Giles, why, they was hot to get rid of the Cassidys. We thought they was just gonna scare 'em. But they set the place on fire and wouldn't let 'em out. Judson and me, we tried to stop it, but they just laughed.'

Dan felt his gut tighten.

'You're swearin' under oath that the three Setons murdered the Cassidy family?' the judge questioned.

'Yes, Your Honor.'

'Judge,' Beeker protested, 'this is all hearsay.'

The judge frowned. 'The testimony of this witness is not hearsay. It's direct testimony and an admission against interest. The charges against Kirk Seton are now to include the murders of the Cassidy family.'

'But, Your Honor, you can't add another charge in the middle of trial.'

'Why not?'

Stumped, Beeker returned to his seat.

'Mr. Hartley,' the judge said, 'can you identify anyone else who was on the raid?'

'No, they all drifted away, Your Honor, except Char Olson. And the marshal got him.'

After Jed returned to his chair, the judge sent the jury to the back room behind the bar. Then he gripped his gavel.

'Marshal, I'll issue a warrant for the Setons as soon as this proceeding ends.'

Dan stood up to turn and look toward the back near the swinging doors. Giles and Karl Seton and their men were gone, leaving Laura alone, her face white. He glanced at Kirk, who had also noticed. Although he was sweating, Kirk held a gleam of hope in his frantic gaze.

The judge continued. 'All charges

against the Hartley brothers are dismissed on all counts. Immunity is granted in regard to the Cassidy murders, given your ages at the time, and since I've been told you've stayed out of trouble until now. You also worked hard to keep your younger brother in college. But I caution you both, you are not to take the law into your own hands ever again.'

The Hartleys looked relieved.

Abruptly, Mace got to his feet at the back of the room, where the Corley brothers were holding him and Buck.

'Your Honor, me and Buck got somethin' to say. It was Char Olson who killed Shanks, 'cause Char was talkin' too much when he was drunk and Shanks overheard. Then Char got Sheriff Denson because he was worried the sheriff would figure it out.'

The judge looked annoyed. 'You're a little late with this confession. Char Olson is dead.'

'But, Your Honor,' Mace urged, 'we oughta get dismissed too for sayin' it.'

'The sentence stands,' the judge said.

Mace was frantic. 'But there's more. Giles Seton, he sent two of his boys to scare that woman at the newspaper. And he paid us to blow up the jail. And what's more, he even paid me and Buck to shut up Creighton . . . '

Mace's voice trailed into a gasp as he realized he had foolishly confessed to murder. Buck kicked at Mace's boot, his mouth twisted in anger. The courtroom burst into laughter. The judge pounded the gavel.

Then the judge leaned forward, eyes gleaming. 'Now then, you want to talk about immunity? I'll entertain it on the Creighton murder if you will both testify against the Setons.'

'Uh, sure,' Mace mumbled.

Kirk glared furiously at them, but he was distracted by the returning jury. Nothing could be read on the faces of the twelve men.

Dan held his breath. For twelve years he had waited to have his family avenged. His heart was pounding, and he glanced at Tex. Any moment, they would know if justice would be done.

The jury foreman stood up slowly.

The judge queried, 'Have you reached a verdict?'

'We have, Your Honor. We find Kirk Seton not guilty of the murder of Josh Hartley.'

The Hartleys looked so angry they were almost bursting, but they didn't move from their chairs.

Then the foreman cleared his throat, and continued.

'Your Honor, we find Kirk Seton guilty of killin' the Cassidy family. We always figured they done it.'

There was a hush in the room as Dan and Tex glanced at each other, tears stinging their eyes, and Dan felt his breath taken away. The judge spoke clearly.

'Kirk Seton, because you were a young man at the time and led by your father, I won't sentence you to hang. Instead, I sentence you to life in Canon City State Prison. You will be transported there as soon as possible.'

Kirk sank in his chair, dumbfounded. He wasn't going to hang, but prison was unacceptable. He half rose, looking around for his father and brother. The crowd suddenly became noisy, whispering and mumbling. Laura Seton hurried outside in tears.

The judge pounded his gavel. 'The courtroom will be cleared immediately. The prisoners will remain. And further, no one is to be out on the street for the next two hours.'

The crowd, the jury, and Beeker reluctantly filtered out into the street and found sanctuary, but the Hartleys remained. The two brothers stood up, faces void of color.

'Your Honor, when the marshal here takes these fellers out into the street, them Setons are gonna be waitin'. We wanta be deputized.'

The judge didn't hesitate. 'Done.'

Dan swore in the Hartleys. Then he nodded to the Corley brothers, who were still holding Mace and Buck. He told them to go across to the jail with the men. 'I figure it's Kirk the Setons will be after,' he explained.

The judge agreed, and the Corleys gave their side arms to the Hartleys, then took Mace and Buck outside. There was no gunfire as they crossed the street.

Hammer stayed behind with Tex, Dan, and the Hartleys. Kirk Seton was sneering with the certain knowledge that his father and brother would be waiting outside the swinging doors.

'I want to warn you,' the judge said to Kirk. 'Your father and brother will be arrested for the Cassidy murders. If they attempt to assure your escape, they will be arrested and possibly shot down in the process.'

'Let 'em do what they want,' Kirk snarled.

Dan and Tex looked toward the swinging doors. They could see that the street had emptied. Yet they knew the Setons and their dozen men were out there, waiting. And the jail was across the street, seemingly a thousand miles away.

If they survived, Tex and Dan would have their horse ranch, somewhere far away from the memories. If they died on the street, at least with their last breath they would know their family would finally rest in peace.

Tex cleared his throat. 'Well, you call it, Dan.'

Dan grabbed Kirk by the arm, bringing him around the chairs and into the aisle. He took the shotgun from Hammer and shoved it into Kirk's belly.

'Let's go, Seton.'

13

It was time.

Tex stood on Kirk's right, gripping his arm. With his hands still cuffed behind his back, Kirk was furious. Dan was on his left, the shotgun shoved into the prisoner's side.

Hammer and the Hartleys skirted them from behind.

Dan kicked open the swinging doors, bringing Kirk into the open. They saw nothing but the empty street, but the silence was heavy and threatening. The door to the jail was open, which worried them.

Giles Seton would try to avoid hurting Kirk, but he surely wanted the others dead, including the judge. He would lose everything, his ranch and his valley, unless he could kill them all.

Dan could almost hear the rancher's hot breath. He glanced at Tex, who had a good grip on the prisoner. He knew Hammer and the Hartleys were behind them and at the windows, scanning the roofs and alleys, watching for any sign.

Suddenly, a rifle bullet shot by Dan's ear.

He and Tex jerked the prisoner back inside.

'Pa,' Kirk shouted, 'get me out of here!'

They moved away from the swinging doors. 'He means to keep us in here,' Tex said grimly.

Dan turned to look at the judge. 'Your Honor, I figure you'd better get out the back way.'

The judge reached inside his black robe and pulled out a long-barreled six-shooter. 'I'm stayin' right here. I got a warrant to issue.'

Suddenly, a barrage of bullets shattered the glass windows on either side of the door. Dan and Tex dragged the prisoner to his knees and away from the windows. Hammer went to the side window, and the Hartleys headed for the back to keep out any intruders.

'They could come in from the upstairs,' Tex said.

'Let's not spread ourselves thin,' Dan responded.

'I got me a bad feelin'.'

Dan nodded. 'Dynamite.'

Kirk looked up with horror. 'No, my pa wouldn't do that. He knows I'm in here.'

'He'll figure you gotta take your chances,' Dan said. 'He wants us dead.'

Abruptly, an unceasing barrage of gunfire riddled the walls and windows. It sounded like a stampede thundering toward them. When it came to a sudden halt, Dan leaned to peer under the swinging doors. He saw Mace diving behind the smithy's trough.

He realized that something had happened to the Corley brothers, and that the prisoners were free. Mace was the one who knew how to use dynamite, and the sticks had been sitting on the office table. Dan began to slide away from the wall.

'Let's get behind the bar.'

Dan and Tex moved hurriedly, dragging Kirk with them. The judge, Hammer, and the Hartleys followed, and they all crouched behind the bar, six-guns and shotgun ready, waiting for the next move.

It came with an explosion that ripped off the front wall of the gambling hall and sent it careening back toward them. Boards and glass and lamps joined tables and chairs. Everything slammed at the bar and crashed on top of them. The smoke and ash and debris had barely settled when a staggering silence followed.

They held their breath, shoving boards off them as they heard running boots on the boardwalk and stairs above.

'Here they come,' Tex whispered.

The gunmen came from the stairs, the landing, the back door, over the fallen front wall. They were firing rapidly, some with six-guns, others with repeating rifles. Mace and Buck kept back with the Setons, ready to move in for the kill. It looked like an army charging through the dust.

The lawmen and the judge fired back. Some of the gunmen fell from the stairs. Others ducked behind tables or parts of the wall. The gunfire was loud and rapid, piercing the bar's exterior like nails being hammered.

Dan couldn't see the Setons. Had they left?

He reloaded his six-gun and crept to the end of the bar, peering out at the debris, seeing a hat at the edge of a table and firing. A man cried out and crashed backward.

Kirk was flat on his belly, squirming and fighting the cuffs behind his back. He was wild, frantic.

Suddenly, there was another explosion. The back wall and part of the ceiling came crashing down on the bar and the room like an avalanche, burying them. They fought to crawl out and yet retain cover.

Gunfire rained on them from all directions.

They fought back, finding the debris a better cover than they had expected. The lawmen cut down Buck, who had pinned them down with a repeater from the stairs. At the same time, Mace leaped through the debris from the back doorway, and Dan hit him square in the chest.

Now it was a fair fight. The lawmen crawled through the debris and scattered. The four remaining gunmen got nervous and started to withdraw.

Abruptly, Karl Seton appeared from the back hallway, shoving aside the broken door and firing rapidly at Dan. A bullet singed by Dan's ear and slammed into a table.

Tex spun and shot Karl in the gut. The man gasped, eyes wild and round. He dropped his gun and grabbed his belly, then fell facedown, dead, on the broken chairs.

Dan looked around. Where was Giles?

The Hartleys and Hammer took care of two of the remaining gunmen, and the judge shot the last, a man whose neck bore long scratches. The echo of the gunfire was still loud, ringing in their ears.

Dan got to his feet. There was only one place left for Giles, and that was out back, trying to get away. He shook off the dirt and debris clinging to him.

He crawled over the door and reloaded his six-gun as he fought his way through the smoke and dust. He staggered outside, just in time to see Giles trying to mount a bucking, nervous horse.

'Seton!'

Giles spun, six-gun in hand. He let go of the horse and fired at Dan, who fired back. The Seton bullet struck Dan hard in the left thigh, but Dan's bullet hit Giles square in the chest.

Giles went down on both knees some ten feet away, staring at Dan, gasping.

'My valley,' the rancher cried.

Dan staggered, trying to balance

himself, his thigh bleeding heavily. He watched the rancher curl up, blood on his chest. The man kept trying to talk, his eyes wild with fury and thirst for revenge.

As Dan watched the rancher die at his feet, all his years of searching for vengeance washed away. He took no pleasure in the man's death. Instead, he felt a strange, cold relief, followed by utter exhaustion.

Giles and Karl Seton were dead, and so were their gunmen. Kirk would spend life in prison with a lot of time to think about what he had done. The Cassidys were avenged.

Dan gazed a long moment at the rancher who had wanted everything at any cost. He almost felt sorry for him. With his hand on his bloody and now painful thigh, he staggered toward the broken back wall.

Tex came out to meet him, putting his arm around him. 'Easy, Dan,' he said.

'It's over, Tex,' Dan said weakly.

'I know. Come on, let's get you to the doctor.'

They paused as the Hartleys and Hammer dragged Kirk outside and let him lie in the fading sunlight. The judge followed. Kirk was dead.

'When the wall caved in,' the judge said, 'it got him and missed us.'

The Hartleys turned to the Cassidys. 'We're right sorry about everything, but there ain't no way we can make it right.'

'You already have,' Dan said, extending his hand.

Jed and Judson shook his hand, then they turned to the judge.

'Your Honor, you kept your word, and we're mighty grateful,' Judson said. 'But now, if you don't mind, I think we just want to go home.'

The judge nodded, watching the two men turn wearily up the alley, shaking the dust from their clothes. Then the jurist turned to the Cassidys.

'It seems justice has been served, Dan. What are your plans now?'

'Ranchin',' Dan said. 'Horses.'

At that moment John Beeker, the merchant who had acted as defense attorney, came over to them.

'Marshal, I was just talkin' with Laura Seton. She wants to sell out and take her mother back East. She said to tell you if you want your old ranch, you could have it back for what it cost her father.'

Startled, Dan swallowed, but a lump stayed in his throat. He looked at Tex. Together they shrugged, uncertain if they could bear the pain of the memories.

'We'd be interested. Maybe,' Dan said quietly.

The judge tugged his beard. 'That would leave just that big fellow, Hammer, to run things.'

'He can handle it,' Dan assured him. 'But he'd like to hear it from you.'

Dan leaned on Tex. 'Well, your gamblin' hall is gone.'

'I keep my money in the Denver bank, so I got plenty to get us goin'. My biggest problem now is Molly. I ain't never wanted a woman so much. She's apple pie and quilts and mornin' sunrise. What if she says no?'

'Don't take no for an answer,' Dan said, his thoughts turning to his own future. Virginia was so wrapped up in her newspaper, maybe she would never want to marry. His face grew hot with worry. Now that he could make a new life, he prayed she would be a part of it.

Tex helped him hobble onto the boardwalk just as Hammer came over to them. The giant looked tired.

'The Corleys got knocked out, but they're all right,' he said.

Relieved, Dan and Tex thanked him and turned away. Dan was dirty, still shaking off dust and debris, and his leg was still bleeding. They headed across the street and down toward the doctor's office.

It was then that they saw Virginia and Molly coming out of a store where they had taken refuge. Both women paused to stare at them.

Dan grinned. 'We're okay.'

Virginia rushed forward, tears running down her face. She put her arm around Dan, helping him away from Tex and toward the doctor's office. Tex drew back and looked at Molly, who was standing with hands on hips and tears flowing.

'Tex Cassidy, you sure gave me a scare.'

'How would you like to keep me out of trouble?'

'What do you mean by that?'

'I mean for life. Get hitched.'

'I don't know anything about you. Do you chaw?'

'Nope.'

'Spit?'

'Nope.'

She smiled through her tears. 'Then I guess you'll do.'

She fell into his arms. He hugged her tight, his heart almost splitting wide open with joy. He kissed her cheek, then her sweet lips. She kissed him back. She felt terrific in his arms, full of life and joy.

Glancing back at Tex and Molly, Virginia was silent. Up in the doctor's office, watching the medic remove the bullet and bandage Dan's thigh, she dried her tears and suddenly turned and went onto the landing.

Dan hobbled after her, catching her arm, but she didn't turn. He felt her quivering at his touch.

'Wait, Virginia. Tex and me, we're goin' to buy a spread, maybe even the old place, start a horse ranch, build a herd. He's figurin' on Molly bein' his wife.'

'I'm glad.'

'But it won't be nothin' without you.'

She turned slowly, a smile crossing her lips. 'What are you saying, Dan Cassidy?'

'Marry me, Virginia.'

She slid her hand into his, her smile so sweet it nearly broke his heart with happiness. Her voice was soft with pleasure, her blue eyes shining.

'What about my newspaper?'

'It's a far piece between it and the ranch.'

'Well, Mr. Beeker's always wanted to buy it, and he would do it proud. And maybe I could help him out now and then.'

'So what do you say?'

'I say you're awful dirty, Dan Cassidy.'

'Will you take me in hand?'

'I thought you'd never ask, Danny.'

She threw her arms around his neck, nearly knocking him over. The pain in his thigh was gone as her lips found his, and he held her to him. And the sound of his nickname on her lips was so welcome it brought tears to his eyes.

Life for the Cassidys was just beginning.

THE END

Lee Phillips is a pseudonym
of Lee Martin who also writes as
Lee Samuels and M. Lemartine.

We do hope that you have enjoyed reading this large print book.

Did you know that all of our titles are available for purchase?

We publish a wide range of high quality large print books including:
Romances, Mysteries, Classics
General Fiction
Non Fiction and Westerns

Special interest titles available in large print are:
The Little Oxford Dictionary
Music Book, Song Book
Hymn Book, Service Book

Also available from us courtesy of Oxford University Press:
Young Readers' Dictionary
(large print edition)
Young Readers' Thesaurus
(large print edition)

For further information or a free brochure, please contact us at:
Ulverscroft Large Print Books Ltd.,
The Green, Bradgate Road, Anstey,
Leicester, LE7 7FU, England.
Tel: (00 44) **0116 236 4325**
Fax: (00 44) **0116 234 0205**

Other titles in the
Linford Western Library:

THE CHISELLER

Tex Larrigan

Soon the paddle-steamer would be on its long journey down the Missouri River to St Louis. Now, all Saul Rhymer had to do was to play the last master-stroke of the evening. He looked at the mounting pile of gold and dollar bills and again at the cards in his hand. Then, looking around the table, he produced the deed to the goldmine in Montana. 'Let's play poker!' But little did he know how that journey back to St Louis would change his life so drastically.

THE ARIZONA KID

Andrew McBride

When former hired gun Calvin Taylor took the job of sheriff of Oxford County, New Mexico, it was for one reason only — to catch, or kill, the notorious Arizona Kid, and pick up the fifteen hundred dollars reward the governor had secretly offered. Taylor found himself on the trail of the infamous gang known as the Regulators, hunting down a man who'd once been his friend. The pursuit became, in every sense, a journey of death.

BULLETS IN BUZZARDS CREEK

Bret Rey

The discovery of a dead saloon girl is only the beginning of Sheriff Jeff Gilpin's problems. Fortunately, his old friend 'Doc' Holliday arrives in Buzzards Creek just as Gilpin is faced by an outlaw gang. In a dramatic shoot-out the sheriff kills their leader and Holliday's reputation scares the hell out of the others. But it isn't long before the outlaws return, when they know Holliday is not around, and Gilpin is alone against six men . . .

THE YANKEE HANGMAN

Cole Rickard

Dan Tate was given a virtually impossible task: to save the murderer Jack Williams from the condemned cell. Williams, scum that he was, held a secret that was dear to the Confederate cause. But if saving Williams would test all Dan's ingenuity, then his further mission called for immense courage and daring. His life was truly on the line and if he didn't succeed, Horace Honeywell, the Yankee Hangman would have the last word!